ALICE WHIPPLE
ON THE CASE

As they neared Madison Avenue, Alice stopped. "Peter! Beatrice! Here!" Alice pulled them down behind a row of garbage cans.

"Not garbage cans again," moaned Peter.

"Shhh!" said Alice. "Look over there!" She pointed to a glassed-in café on the corner. "It's the two suspects," she whispered.

"Hey, that's Miss Slade!" Beatrice shouted.

"Shh! Keep your voice down."

"I don't think they can hear us through the glass, Alice," Peter said.

"You never know. They might have hidden microphones. Notice, Peter, that they are obviously plotting. They're leaning over the table."

"I think they're having lunch," Peter said.

"Peter, anyone can see how suspicious that man is. He has a beard, *and* he's wearing dark glasses."

"My uncle has a beard," Peter said. "So did Abraham Lincoln."

Soon Miss Slade and the man with the beard rose from the table. They left the café arm in arm.

"Look!" Alice said. "There's another man, and he's following them!"

They watched a man in a shiny, black, belted raincoat.

"It's not raining, Beatrice. And it is therefore significant that he is wearing a raincoat." Alice gave her sister a punch on the arm.

"Ouch! What was that for?" Beatrice was outraged.

"So you'll *remember.* This is a major clue. And I don't want you to forget it!"

Other Bantam Skylark Books you'll enjoy

ALICE WHIPPLE, FIFTH-GRADE DETECTIVE

LAURIE ADAMS
and
ALLISON COUDERT

A BANTAM SKYLARK BOOK®
TORONTO · NEW YORK · LONDON · SYDNEY · AUCKLAND

RL 4, 008–012

ALICE WHIPPLE, FIFTH-GRADE DETECTIVE
A Bantam Book / May 1987

Skylark Books is a registered trademark of Bantam Books, Inc.
Registered in U.S. Patent and Trademark Office and elsewhere.

ISBN 0-553-15485-0

Published simultaneously in the United States and Canada

Bantam Books are published by Bantam Books, Inc. Its trademark, consisting of the words "Bantam Books" and the por-
trayal of a rooster, is registered in U.S. Patent and Trademark
Office and in other countries. Marca Registrada. Bantam
Books, Inc., 666 Fifth Avenue, New York, New York 10103.

PRINTED IN THE UNITED STATES OF AMERICA

O   0 9 8 7 6 5 4 3 2

To Alexa, Caroline, and Polly

CONTENTS

CHAPTER ONE

INDECISION

"What on earth is the matter, Alice?" Mr. Whipple asked his daughter, who was staring glumly at her taco. "You're not eating." Tacos were Alice's favorite food.

"She's too dumb to do her English homework," Beatrice, Alice's younger sister, piped up between bites.

"Alice is not dumb, dear," Mrs. Whipple said.

The Whipple family was having dinner. Gerald Whipple worked on Wall Street in New York City, and Mary, his wife, was a part-time reading teacher. She liked to be home in the afternoons when her two daughters were out of school. They attended Miss Barton's School for Girls, a private school on East Eighty-first Street. Alice was in the fifth grade, and Beatrice was a first grader.

"Just what *is* your homework?" Mr. Whipple inquired. He took the girls' homework very seriously. "Is it something we could discuss together?"

"Our English teacher is such a jerk! She gave us only one night to write a whole essay. It's not fair!" Alice nudged a piece of onion from her taco shell and pushed it around her plate with her fork.

"What's the subject of the essay?" her mother asked.

"She has to say what she wants to be when she grows up. And she doesn't know," Beatrice pronounced, her short blond hair and bangs bouncing as she emphatically nodded her head.

"Oh, shut up!" Alice stormed, her identically cut blond hair brushing her face as she glared at her sister. "You don't know anything about it."

Beatrice never had homework because at Miss Barton's homework didn't start until the fourth grade.

"I have to write an essay called 'My Future Career,'" Alice informed her parents. "And I have to explain *why* I chose that career. Everyone else did the essay in study hall this afternoon. They all know what they're going to be. I'm the only one who doesn't know," Alice wailed.

"Actually, that's a very good assignment," Mr. Whipple pointed out. "There have been a lot of great women in history. You could use some of them as models for your essay." He paused and sipped his water. "There was Cleopatra, the famous queen of Egypt. And Elizabeth the First of England. She inspired poets and explorers and Shakespeare—I guess you won't read Shakespeare until you're older, but you could mention him."

"Shakespeare wasn't a woman," Alice said.

"And Queen Victoria," Mr. Whipple continued. "She dominated an entire age and style in England. Or, if you prefer, there was Catherine the Great of Russia."

"I think she had her husband murdered to get the throne," Mrs. Whipple said.

Alice squirmed in her seat. "Those are all queens. I can't be a queen, Daddy. Not unless you are a king."

Mr. Whipple was a banker.

"And besides," Alice informed her father, "being a queen is not exactly a career. I need a career."

"You could be a tightrope walker in the circus," Beatrice said cheerfully. She had finished her dinner, so she was now concentrating solely on Alice's problem. Beatrice was in an afternoon gymnastics program, along with her best friend, Emily.

"Bor-r-r-ing!" said Alice. "And I'd get big, ugly muscles."

"Well, if you think it's so boring, you could be a tightrope walker without a net. Then it'd be exciting."

"What about being a scientist?" Mrs. Whipple suggested. "Like Marie Curie." Mrs. Whipple knew that science was Alice's favorite subject. "She discovered radium and won two Nobel prizes. If it hadn't been for her, we wouldn't have X-ray machines today."

"I had an X ray when I broke my arm," Beatrice observed.

"That's what you get for doing gymnastics," Alice retorted.

Beatrice was still thinking about the circus. "You could be the fat lady in the circus. Then you'd never have to exercise again. You could skip gym and just eat. Mrs. Tully would probably give you a permanent gym excuse if you told her you were going to be the fat lady in the circus."

Mrs. Tully was the school nurse. She was very popular with the girls because she was terribly sympathetic to their ailments, real or imagined. Mrs. Tully was less popular with the gym department.

"Oh, shut up, Beatrice!" Alice said again.

Beatrice had hit upon a sensitive subject. She stayed slim no matter how much she ate, and Alice thought it was extremely unfair because *she* still had a tiny bit of baby fat.

Alice decided to ignore Beatrice. She returned to the subject of Marie Curie. "Marie Curie died of radiation poisoning," Alice told her mother. "We learned that in science class."

Mrs. Whipple tried a different approach. "Margaret Mead was another famous woman. And she led an exciting life. She was an anthropologist."

"What's an anthropologist?" Alice asked.

"If you divide the word into two sections," Mr. Whipple explained, "you can figure it out. 'Anthrop' comes from the Greek word for 'human being or man' and 'ology' means 'the study of something.'"

"Like biology," Alice said.

"Exactly." Her father had studied Greek and Latin before he became a banker. "Therefore," continued Mr. Whipple, "anthropology is the study of man."

"Alice is going to study men?" Beatrice asked, perking up. "What kind of men? Is she going to X-ray them?"

"No, silly," her mother said and smiled at her. "Anthropologists study whole families and cultures and societies. Margaret Mead lived in remote places, like Samoa and New Guinea, where the people haven't developed modern technology. That means no machines or telephones—"

"No computers?" Alice was alarmed. "How can

anyone *live* without a computer?" Alice thought of her Apple IIe.

"It would be like camping out," added Mr. Whipple. "You enjoyed your camping weekend, didn't you, Alice? Anthropologists sometimes live in tents or mud huts."

"Alice couldn't live without a telephone. How would she talk to Peter?" Beatrice wondered out loud.

Peter Hildreth lived in the apartment building across the street. He and his younger brother, James, were in the same grades as Alice and Beatrice, but they attended the local public school.

"Wel-l-l-l." Alice wasn't sure.

"There are probably a lot of jungles in those places," Beatrice pointed out. "You'd have to look out for the poisonous animals—toads, and snakes, and cockroaches, and piranha fish. If you put your foot in a river with piranha fish only your bones come out."

"Please, Beatrice," Mr. Whipple said. "We are trying to have a serious discussion."

"But this *is* serious. You have to be careful. I check my salad every day at lunch for cockroaches."

Alice confirmed that the school lunches were not ideal. Her best friend, Sarah, had found two cockroaches in her salad the week before.

"Well," Mrs. Whipple said, "part of adjusting to another culture means learning to eat their food."

"And I bet they have cannibals, too." Beatrice had clearly not exhausted the subject of anthropology. "They shrink your head. In fact," said Beatrice. "Marina's head is a bit big. Maybe *she* should be an anthrop-whatever."

"Ologist," Alice finished. Marina was one of Alice's

classmates. She was quite tall for her age. And even
though she was a Peach like Alice, she was not one of
Alice's favorites. The fifth grade at Miss Barton's was
divided into two groups, the Peaches and the Turnips.
Alice had been a Peach since the fourth grade. Miss
Barton's did not approve of cliques, so the students had to
keep their groups secret.

Mr. and Mrs. Whipple could see that anthropology
wouldn't suit Alice. Mrs. Whipple started clearing away the
dinner dishes. There wasn't much time left for Alice to
decide on her topic.

"What about literature?" Mr. Whipple suggested.
"There are a lot of good women writers."

"Writer?" Beatrice interrupted. "She can't even write an
English essay!"

Mr. Whipple ignored Beatrice. "Sappho was an early
Greek poet," he said. "And Jane Austen wrote *Pride and
Prejudice,* and there were the Brontë sisters—"

"*Frankenstein* was written by a woman," Mrs. Whipple
added, returning to the dining room.

"You could make a monster, Alice." Beatrice beamed.
"And he could kill all the Turnips."

"Oh, shut up! Daddy, can't you make her shut up?"

"Please be quiet, Beatrice!" her father said.

Beatrice cried.

"Beatrice," her mother said sternly, "go and get the
chocolate-chip ice cream out of the freezer, take the top
off, and watch it get soft. Call me when it's ready."

Beatrice couldn't resist a good dish of chocolate-chip
ice cream, so she went, sniffling.

"There was Emily Dickinson, Elizabeth Barrett Browning, George Eliot, and George Sand," Mr. Whipple continued.

"George?" Beatrice called out from the kitchen.

"George was a pseudonym," her father explained. "They used men's names even though they were women."

"But why?" Alice was curious. "What was wrong with their own names?"

"Nothing was wrong with them," her mother replied. "But everyone thought that readers would prefer a male author."

"That's ridiculous," Alice said. "*Gone with the Wind* was written by a woman and our whole class is reading it."

"No one believes that men authors are better than women anymore," her father said. "Nowadays, women can do anything."

"In that case," Beatrice said as she emerged from the kitchen, "she can be a doorwoman, a garbage woman, or a snowwoman."

"Back in the kitchen, Beatrice."

"But it's not soft yet."

"Go back and watch it," her father ordered.

"I need something exciting," Alice said. "Something adventurous. Like Amelia Earhart did. I could fly an airplane, see the world, take a lot of pictures, meet different people—"

"I saw a movie about her with James," Beatrice called out from her post by the chocolate-chip ice cream. "She never came back from her last flight. I bet her plane crashed and she drowned in the ocean and the piranha fish ate her."

"The ice cream, Beatrice!" Her father spoke very slowly between clenched teeth. "Alice, have you ever thought of a career as a wife and mother? I bet no one at Miss Barton's ever thought of that. Look at that poster of a mother and child by Mary Cassatt," Mr. Whipple said, pointing to the reproduction from the Metropolitan Museum of Art hanging on the dining room wall. "Mary Cassatt was an American who went to Paris to study with the impressionists in the nineteenth century. Mothers and children were her favorite subjects."

Alice looked at the poster for a few moments.

"That's it!" she said. "I'll be an artist! I'll go to France and learn French and be a famous painter. Our French teacher says you have to live in France to really get your ear used to the language. French food is good, too."

"You got a C in art last year," Beatrice screamed from the kitchen.

"You can bring in the ice cream now," her mother said. "And don't forget the dishes and spoons."

"How come Alice doesn't have to do anything?"

"All geniuses are misunderstood," said Alice, referring to her C in art. "Some painters never sell their pictures. We have art tomorrow afternoon. I'll begin my career tomorrow."

"After you write your paper tonight," said her father.

CHAPTER TWO

SECOND THOUGHTS

Alice decided to skip afternoon recess because she wanted to get to art class early. She planned to start her new career by helping Miss Slade, the art instructor.

Alice entered the seventh floor art room. It was an enormous rectangular room with three floor-to-ceiling windows on one side. The room was filled with flamboyant still life displays. An enormous white, porcelain fruit bowl shared a tabletop with a pyramid of squashes, gourds, and pumpkins. Variously shaped vases were filled with dried marsh grass, cattails and pussy willows. A life-size mannequin lay stretched out on a leather divan. It was dressed in a flowing, white robe, which Miss Slade had brought back from a trip to Tunisia. She called it a "jelab." The mannequin's head was covered in a snowy white turban with a large fake ruby pinned in the middle.

To the right of the divan was a standing mannequin, a woman in a beige, silk Victorian dress with a huge bustle and a matching silk hat and parasol. The mannequin wore an elaborate pearl necklace with a large emerald pendant that matched her emerald earrings. More costume jewelry

9

filled an open box on a nearby table. Miss Slade would change the mannequin's jewelry for variety. The students in the older grades studied the jewelry when they did paintings of reflections.

A bust of Nefertiti, a famous Egyptian queen, stood on the table next to the box of costume jewelry. Around her neck was a gold necklace with bands of blue lapis lazuli, the favorite semiprecious stone of the Egyptian pharaohs.

Miss Slade kept all the art materials at one end of the room. Jars of paint cluttered the top of a row of cabinets, which held brushes, crayons, markers, pencils, pens, and stacks of various types and sizes of paper. Big containers of clay and plaster filled the lower shelves. In a far corner four pottery wheels were lined up next to the kiln.

Miss Slade was perched on a ladder at the opposite end of the room. Her back was toward the door. Her hair was pulled back into a single, black braid, which hung down to her waist. All the girls at Miss Barton's knew that Miss Slade dyed her hair because some days it had more gray than others. She was tall and thin. That day she was wearing a long mustard-colored skirt and a white peasant blouse with huge sleeves. Alice heard her bracelets clank as she picked through objects on the high shelves. Her Swedish clogs waited for her at the foot of the ladder.

"Hi, Miss Slade."

At the sound of Alice's voice, Miss Slade turned abruptly, almost dropping the statue of an owl, which she held in one hand. The ladder swayed dangerously, and Alice rushed over to steady it.

"Gracious, Alice, you startled me!" Miss Slade certainly looked startled.

"I'm sorry, Miss Slade." Alice really was. Miss Slade

was known for her bad temper, and Alice hadn't the least desire to begin her career with a terrible disaster. She could see the headlines now: "Art Teacher Knocked Unconscious by Schoolgirl." Her career would be ruined before it had even begun!

"I thought you heard me come in, or I would have said something. Last night I decided to be an artist. So I thought I'd come by early to help you set up. I want to learn everything I can."

"What a good idea, Alice." Miss Slade had regained her composure. "The last class didn't get all the paint out of their brushes. Take them over to the sink and see if you can get it out. You know, it's a good idea to start with the basics. And while you are busy doing that, I'll take down these owls and arrange them."

Alice's class had spent the past three weeks doing pencil drawings of owls. That day they were going to paint in the drawings.

"Okay, Miss Slade." Alice hoped Miss Slade didn't hear the disappointment in her voice. She had a horrible feeling that things weren't going to turn out the way she had expected. Would it always be the same? When she had told her mother she wanted to learn to cook, her mother had given her the lettuce to wash!

Alice suppressed a sigh and picked up the brushes. On her way to the sink, she passed the displays. *Funny,* she thought, stopping and peering into the fruit bowl. She craned her neck to one side and bent down. Yes, the apple had at least six worm holes! And the banana was all brown. Alice knew for a fact that one melon had been there since the beginning of the year. The outside was all wrinkly. She hated to imagine what the inside was like.

"Is something the matter, Alice?"

Alice straightened up. She turned and saw Miss Slade. She had come down from the ladder and was arranging the owls on a table in the middle of the circle of easels. The owls were of different colors—black, brown, yellow, red, and green. Some had open wings and some closed. They all had wide, staring eyes.

"No, Miss Slade." Alice didn't want to mention the fruit. Miss Slade was very touchy about her displays. In fact, she got very angry if anyone tampered with them. She called the art room her "little kingdom."

Alice went over to the sink. She turned on the tap and began washing the brushes with Mr. Clean and cold water. She was sure that more than one class hadn't cleaned them properly. It seemed like hours before her classmates began filing in.

"Hi, Alice. See you got K.P. That's short for Kitchen Patrol." Hilary's uncle was an army general, so she was always using military terms to show how smart she was. Even though Hilary was a Peach, Alice thought she was a snob.

"Oh, hello, Hilary." Alice nodded. She didn't feel like discussing what she was doing with anyone, least of all Hilary. Hilary's brown hair flounced as she walked past Alice toward the cabinets where the drawings were kept.

"I do wish we could draw something decent like horses," Hilary whispered. "Owls are so boring. Miss Barton's should have a horse for a mascot, not an owl." Hilary was an expert rider because she had taken riding lessons since she was three years old. "There are too many owls at this school as it is."

Everything was boring to Hilary, except horses, Alice

thought. But she had to admit that about the owls Hilary was right.

When Miss Barton had founded the school in 1884, she had decided on the owl as the school emblem. It was a symbol of the wisdom she hoped to instill in her students. In ancient Greece the owl represented Athena, the goddess of wisdom, who was called "owl-eyed" by the poets. Each class had its own stuffed owl mascot that stayed with the class from kindergarten through the twelfth grade. Every year the graduating class passed its owl on to the incoming kindergarten class.

Alice noticed that Hilary was wearing her school uniform properly for a change. Mrs. Partridge, the headmistress, had cracked down on the school dress code the week before, so Hilary couldn't wear jodhpurs, even if she did have a riding lesson after school. Mrs. Partridge had, in fact, been quite specific about the dress code. She had sent a circular to all the parents detailing just what was and was not acceptable. Aside from shirts having to have collars, underwear was not permitted over the school uniform. And jewelry was definitely frowned upon. So was makeup. But Alice happened to know that Hilary couldn't resist jewelry and that every day she wore a pearl necklace with a real sapphire in the center under her blouse.

Alice was glad when Wing Chu, Lydia, Jennifer, and some of the other girls arrived. Soon the class would start, and she could stop washing caked brushes.

"What are you doing, Alice?" Lydia asked. Lydia had long black hair tied back in a ponytail. Lydia was a good friend of Hilary, but Alice preferred Lydia because she wasn't as snobby as Hilary.

"I wonder myself." Alice was beginning to have second thoughts about her art career. Alice also wondered where Sarah was. It was almost time for class to begin. Sarah was never late. Sarah Jamison was Alice's best friend.

"All right, girls." Miss Slade clapped her hands for attention. Her bracelets jangled. "I want all of you to find your pictures and start working. Today we will begin painting our owl drawings. Paint with *broad* strokes and *bold* colors. I want you to let your imaginations soar like these owls.

"This will be your first experience with acrylic paint. Acrylic is a versatile medium. You can make it look like oil paint or watercolor depending on how much you thin it." Miss Slade's gold bracelets clanked again as she waved her arms in the air like a pair of wings. Her dangling gold earrings glittered in the sunlight pouring through the windows. "Remember, a child's imagination is beyond all imagination!"

That was one of Miss Slade's favorite sayings. Alice knew it by heart. She also knew what was coming next. "Art and imagination. These are what we strive for in this classroom. Imagination *not* technique!"

Alice wasn't sure what Miss Slade meant by "technique." She remembered once when Miss Slade made Wing Chu paint out all the shading in one of her pictures. Shading was probably "technique."

The class settled down to work. Alice decided to use red, green, and gold for her owl painting. She planned to give it to her parents as a Christmas present.

Miss Slade turned on a tape of classical music to help the class concentrate.

Alice was wondering if yellow was the right color for

the eyes when the door to the art room burst open and Sarah breathlessly rushed in, her red curls bouncing.

"I'm sorry to be late, Miss Slade," Sarah apologized.

"Sarah, you're breaking the class's concentration. I will hear your excuses later. Just find your picture and commence painting."

Sarah walked toward the cabinet as the class settled back to work.

Suddenly Sarah blurted out. "My picture—it's gone! I can't find it! I spent weeks on it. What will I do now?" Sarah wailed.

"What do you mean?" Miss Slade clomped over to the cabinets, moving faster than Alice thought possible. "Your picture couldn't be gone, Sarah. They are all right here." First she checked the shelf reserved for that class and then she turned to face them.

All eyes were on Miss Slade. Alice had never seen her so flustered. Her face was bright red. Alice wasn't sure why she was so upset. But artists were supposed to be temperamental and Miss Slade certainly was.

"Somebody in this school is untrustworthy! Somebody has been in *my* art room!" Miss Slade cast a steely glance around the room. "This is most distressing," she said.

Alice groaned to herself. She was sure they would have to spend the rest of the class looking through all the cabinets for the missing owl drawing. She was relieved when Miss Slade dismissed the class early.

Alice was the last to leave the art room. She heard the door shut behind her.

CHAPTER THREE

A TRIP TO THE MUSEUM

Alice's section of her fifth grade class stood in the coat check line at the Metropolitan Museum of Art. The class had taken the Eighty-sixth Street crosstown bus from East End Avenue after their first period class. Mrs. Parker, the fifth-grade homeroom teacher, was accompanying Miss Slade and the girls to an exhibit of pre-Columbian gold. Miss Slade had obtained special permission for the class to bring sketch pads and pencils to draw the objects. Mrs. Parker would discuss the history of the objects before the girls sketched. The class was studying the Spanish conquest of the New World in its history unit.

"Pssst, Sarah!" Alice nudged her best friend, who stood next to her in the line. "Look over there." Alice nodded toward the information desk.

Sarah turned and saw Miss Slade talking to a tall, dark man with a beard. He wore a gray suit and dark glasses. He and Miss Slade were deep in conversation.

"Gosh, Alice," Sarah whispered.

17

"Do you see what they're doing?" Alice watched as the man handed Miss Slade a brown paper bag, which she quickly dropped into her wide straw handbag.

"And over there, Sarah. Look over there at that man holding a black hat and raincoat. He's staring at Miss Slade."

"Come on, girls," Mrs. Parker urged. "We have to keep moving. Our appointment in the pre-Columbian gallery started five minutes ago."

A short time later the class was assembled in front of the display cases. They were filled with gold objects: statues of animals, primitive gods, and elaborate necklaces, bracelets, and earrings. At the entrance to the gallery, a guard watched nervously as the children pressed up against the glass cases.

"Not too close, girls," Miss Slade warned, smiling at the guard. She had rejoined the class.

"These are the kinds of objects that were made in South America before Columbus came to the New World," Mrs. Parker explained. "As you know, Columbus's exploration was financed by the Spanish, even though he was Italian."

"But—" Wing Chu raised her hand— "Columbus wasn't even looking for America. He was looking for India and China. He discovered America by mistake."

"That's right," Mrs. Parker said. "The Europeans wanted spices and gold from Asia. Later they came to exploit the Americas. Do you remember the story of Ponce de Leon? We read about him last week. He went looking for the Fountain of Youth, which was believed to be in Florida."

Alice thought Mrs. Parker looked quite youthful herself in her bright green Nike running shoes.

"Did he ever find the fountain?" asked Marina. "My mother is always trying new face creams. She says they make her skin look younger."

Yuck! Alice thought to herself. Marina was forever asking about makeup. She was the tallest girl in the class and was very interested in boys.

"My father says a lot of those face products are dangerous," said Sarah, whose father was an advertising executive.

"No," said Mrs. Parker. "I don't think he did find a fountain. We would have heard of it. But there was something else the Spanish came for. Does anyone know?" She paused. No one raised her hand. "As soon as they discovered South America, the Spanish heard tales of the mythical city of Eldorado. They believed that Eldorado was made completely of gold. Even the streets were said to be paved with it. No one is sure where Eldorado was supposed to be or even if it ever really existed. But there was so much gold in South America that the story seemed possible.

"South American gold became legendary, and the Spanish explorers were eager to take back as much of it as they could. These displays give you some idea of what was available. For example, look at these discs." Mrs. Parker pointed to several plain, round gold discs in the case on her right. "These are called pectoral discs. Pectoral comes from the Latin word for chest. If you look closely, you can see small holes in the discs. Cords decorated with shells, beads, and feathers were strung through these holes and used to tie the discs in place—like breast plates."

Marina's hand shot up. "Do you mean that men wore bras in those days?"

Alice groaned and exchanged glances with Sarah. Marina thought she was so great because she was the only girl in the fifth grade who wore a bra.

"No, Marina," Mrs. Parker replied. "Pectorals aren't bras. They were worn for decoration." Mrs. Parker continued her history lesson. "When Columbus made his fourth voyage along the coast of Costa Rica and Panama in 1502, he reported seeing Indians wearing 'mirrors' of gold as neck ornaments. They were probably discs like these. Spanish explorers described a golden garden they had seen in the Inca capital of Cuzco. The earth was made up of fine pieces of gold, and the garden was planted with golden corn. The stalks, leaves, and corn kernels were all made of gold."

"They must have been awfully rich," Hilary said. "I bet they had lots of horse races and wore tons of jewelry."

"Like those nose ornaments," said Alice, pointing to a case on the far wall. "They're so huge you wouldn't be able to talk or eat if you wore one." Alice thought they'd look great on Hilary, but she decided not to say so.

"Girls, girls, let's stay on the subject." Mrs. Parker called for attention. "Gold was not the only thing of value in South America." She turned to the next case. "These gold owls, for example." Mrs. Parker pointed to a group of four golden owls with bright green eyes. "Notice that their eyes are made of emeralds. South America had emeralds as well as gold. One of the Eldorado legends tells of five golden owls with jeweled eyes that were hidden from the

Spanish by Montezuma, the Aztec king. When archae-
ologists found five owls that fitted the legendary descrip-
tion, they thought that they had stumbled upon Eldorado.
But apparently not. Either there was no Eldorado after all,
or the owls had been moved. There were only five of these
owls, although many copies exist. Four of the originals are
right here. The fifth should have been, too, but it was
stolen the first day it arrived here at the museum. Perhaps
some of you heard about the theft."

Lydia waved her hand back and forth. "I did, Mrs.
Parker. They said it was worth a fortune. I bet the C.I.A.,
the F.B.I., and Interpol are all looking for it." Lydia thought
she was an expert on spies and undercover operations.
She never missed a James Bond movie.

"These owls look just like *my* owl," Alice said
suddenly. "The one I'm copying for my art project."

"Yes, they do," Miss Slade agreed. "That's very
perceptive of you. You have a good eye. Fortunately this
museum has a big reproduction section in the gift shop, so
I was able to get several copies of these owls for the art
room. They aren't as dazzling, especially without the
emerald eyes, but they have the same beautiful shapes. It
is important to study works of art from the past as well as
to draw from nature. In fact"—she turned to Mrs. Parker—
"maybe we should begin sketching. There's not too much
time left."

The class settled down to sketch. Each student picked
an object and began to draw.

"If that isn't just like Hilary," Alice whispered to Sarah.
"Trust her to pick a necklace. All she cares about is jewelry
and horses."

"I can't get this mask to look right," groaned Marina.

"The nose is lopsided. It's not even very good-looking."

Alice nudged Sarah. "Look at Miss Slade. She's leaving."

"So? Maybe she's going to the ladies' room."

"Sarah, be serious. Something is going on."

"Be quiet, Alice. I'm trying to concentrate on my drawing."

But Alice wasn't satisfied. She tried to draw one of the little gods, but she was distracted. *I know that something odd is happening,* Alice told herself. *I'll show Sarah. You'd think Sarah would realize that something's wrong,* Alice thought. *After all, yesterday her owl disappeared. And today Miss Slade gets a package from a suspicious-looking man with a beard. And now she's leaving the group for the second time in one morning. Somehow this is all connected. It's up to me to find the missing link.*

Alice was still having trouble with the little god she was trying to draw. He had geometric arms that stuck out from the sides in a zig-zag fashion. *Maybe I'm not cut out to be an artist after all,* she thought. *Maybe I'd be a better detective. A good detective would keep an eye on Miss Slade.*

Alice stopped sketching and asked Mrs. Parker if she could be excused to go to the ladies' room.

"All right, Alice," Mrs. Parker said. She glanced at her watch. "But be sure to be back in ten minutes. We'll have to be going by then. I'll meet you at the coat check line."

"Yes, Mrs. Parker."

Alice folded up her sketch pad and tucked her Miss Barton's pencil behind her ear. She took off in the same direction as Miss Slade. Alice hurried past the information desk and caught sight of Miss Slade going toward the

Greek and Roman galleries. Alice slowed down and kept a safe distance behind her. Miss Slade continued past the Roman sarcophagi in the middle of the hall between the two rooms of Greek sculpture. *This is the way to the cafeteria,* Alice said to herself. *I wonder why she's going this way.* Suddenly a tour guide, followed by a line of tourists, emerged from one of the Greek rooms. They blocked Alice's view of Miss Slade.

Now what? Alice thought. *I'll never find her.* Frantically, Alice ran around the tourists. By the time she passed them, Miss Slade was gone. Alice quickly dashed into the cafeteria, checking the tables and the lunch line. Nothing. She glanced at the people seated in the sunken restaurant in the middle of the cafeteria. No Miss Slade. A waiter stared at Alice. *I must look suspicious,* she thought.

She knew she had to do something. The ladies' room! It was right by the cafeteria entrance.

As long as she was there, Alice decided she would use the ladies' room. Obviously the tourists had had the same idea, so Alice had to stand in line. It was a long line, and she was stuck behind a fat woman with a noisy little boy. He was obviously too young to go anywhere alone, so there he was with his mother standing in line in the Metropolitan Museum of Art ladies' room in front of Alice. He stuck his tongue out at her. He had chocolate on his mouth and an ugly scab on his chin. Alice made a face at him and wiggled her ears. He cried.

Then Alice saw Miss Slade enter the ladies' room. But she didn't stand in line. She excused herself and went straight over to the row of sinks and stood looking in the mirror.

Alice was fascinated, but she had to turn toward the

wall so Miss Slade wouldn't recognize her. Alice studied the graffiti on the wall intently. "Raymond loves Lucy" was scrawled across a wobbly heart with an arrow through it. Out of the corner of her eye, Alice kept tabs on Miss Slade.

Miss Slade plopped her large straw handbag on the rim of the sink. She removed the paper bag that the bearded man had given her and carefully took out what was inside and stuffed the bag into the trash can.

Alice watched.

Miss Slade held up a long gold necklace in front of the mirror. The necklace looked like the ones in the exhibit. Embedded in the gold were a lot of green stones. Alice knew they must be emeralds. Miss Slade smiled. Definitely sinister, thought Alice. Miss Slade never smiled. Even odder, Miss Slade put the necklace on and tied her fringed shawl around her neck. Alice tried to snuggle up behind the fat woman so Miss Slade wouldn't recognize her uniform. Fortunately, Miss Slade was so pleased with her reflection that she didn't notice anyone else. She then left the ladies' room.

Alice was thinking hard. She knew that she was on to something big and important. Miss Slade had definitely acted in a suspicious manner. It was clear to Alice that Miss Slade was smuggling the necklace out of the museum. Why else would she hide it under her shawl?

Alice felt certain that she had finally discovered her true vocation. How else would she have known enough to enter the ladies' room after she had lost her suspect and then have it turn out that her suspect entered the ladies' room just after her? Clearly, Alice thought, she had the right instincts to be a detective. She would be famous. She was on the verge of a major breakthrough. She had stumbled onto an international ring of jewel thieves operating right there in the Metropolitan Museum of Art, and Miss Slade was at the very heart of the operation!

Alice might even be the youngest detective in the *Guinness Book of World Records*. She imagined her entry.

Alice Whipple: youngest female detective in history. Cracked her first case—The Case of the International Jewel Ring—at the age of ten.

Alice made up her mind. She would be a detective. Art would be her hobby. After all, Sherlock Holmes played the violin in his spare time.

CHAPTER FOUR

THE PLOT THICKENS

On Saturday morning Alice sat at her desk, deep in concentration. She was feeding clues into her Apple IIe. Alice typed *110 Print Suspects* just as Peter Hildreth burst into her room.

Alice jumped. "Peter! *Never* do that again!"

"Come on, Alice. It's great out today. Let's go roller-skating."

"How did you get in here, anyway?"

"I rang the buzzer downstairs, your mother answered it, and I came up. The usual way. Your mother said she thinks you need some fresh air."

"Don't be silly, Peter. I'm involved in a very serious and important project. I can't be disturbed."

Peter strolled around to Alice's side of the desk. He didn't have a computer. His parents disapproved of them. They thought that reading books and turning pages were better than pushing buttons and staring at electronic screens.

"How do you work that thing?" Peter inquired casually, hoping Alice couldn't tell how interested he was.

"It takes a lot of practice," Alice said. "You have to spend a lot of time on it before you're as good as I am."

"Alice!" Mrs. Whipple called out.

"Now what?"

"Alice!" her mother called again. "It's Sarah! She's on the phone. She needs the math assignment."

"I'll be right back, Peter. Don't you dare touch a thing. If you do, you might accidently turn it off and then my whole program will disappear."

Peter nodded. He looked out the window. "Okay, Alice. But hurry up. We want to get out and skate."

"*You* want to skate, Peter. Not me." Alice rushed from her room.

"Listen, Peter. I might be willing to let you help me with my project," Alice said when she came back to her room.

She had decided that Peter might be useful. After all, didn't Sherlock Holmes have Watson, didn't Hercule Poirot have Hastings? Even Miss Marple had her old friend from St. Mary's Mead to discuss her cases with.

"Oh?" said Peter as Alice sat down at her computer. He looked over her shoulder.

Alice called up her document file entitled Suspects.

"What are you doing, Alice?"

"It's top secret, Peter. If I told you, you would have to promise not to tell anyone, not a single, solitary soul. Not even James."

"That's what you said last summer when you thought Mrs. Miller was a Russian spy."

Mrs. Miller was the little old lady who lived down the street. Every day she took her miniature white French poodle, Queen Anne's Lace, for a walk. And every day they would meet a friend.

"You told me she and the man she talked to were trading government secrets while they sat on the bench. Do you remember, Alice? We followed them, and you hid behind a tree. *I* had to crouch by the garbage cans on the corner. They really smelled. It was a hot day, too. Boy, was that disgusting! And all they talked about was their false teeth."

I still think that might've been a code," Alice declared, staring straight at her computer screen. "If I'd had my Apple IIe then, I bet I could've cracked the code. But this is different, Peter."

"Different? How?"

"This requires careful planning. We have to reconstruct the crime by studying the suspects and the clues."

"Oh?" Peter was beginning to sound interested.

"Yes. Now look at the screen. When I run my Suspects program, the computer prints out the list of suspects." Alice typed *Run* and pressed Enter.

Peter saw;

<u>SUSPECTS</u>
MISS SLADE
THE BEARD

appear on the screen.

"There are only two suspects," he pointed out.

"That's because I've narrowed them down. Now, watch this." And Alice ran the Clues program.

Peter looked at the screen again.

CLUES .

SARAH'S STOLEN OWL
BROWN PAPER BAG
SLADE HIDES NECKLACE UNDER SHAWL

"There are only three clues," Peter said.

"But they are *extremely* significant clues," Alice insisted. "An experienced detective can sometimes solve a case with only one clue. It's the significance of the clue that counts. Besides, if you decide to help me, I *might* agree to roller-skate with you. *If* you agreed first to come with me to the Metropolitan Museum to investigate."

The Whipples lived on Eighty-eighth Street between Park and Madison, so it was only a few blocks to the museum. But even so, Alice wasn't allowed to skate that far.

"Investigate what?" Peter asked.

"The suspects, Peter. You're not paying attention."

"But what do you suspect them *of*, Alice?"

"Swear you won't tell anyone?"

"Swear."

"Okay." Alice took a deep breath and told Peter about Sarah's missing owl picture and Miss Slade and the museum trip. She explained the clues and her theory about the international ring of jewel thieves.

"You wouldn't think they'd have jewel thieves at a school like Miss Barton's," Peter said. He and James often teased Alice and Beatrice because they went to a private school and had to wear uniforms. Peter and James called Alice and Beatrice Miss Barton's Brats because of the yellow *B* on their school blazers. And sometimes they called them Barton's Birds because of the owl stitched on the pocket.

"That's not the point, Peter. If you're going to help me, you have to concentrate. Shhh!" Alice motioned suddenly. "What was that noise?"

"I didn't hear anything."

"Keep talking," Alice whispered. She got up and tiptoed over to her closet. She yanked open the door. Beatrice fell out onto the floor.

"Beatrice! How dare you!"

"I want to roller-skate with you."

"You can't."

"That's not fair!"

"Out!" Alice shoved Beatrice to her door. "Go away."

Alice was collecting her skates from the box of miscellaneous objects by the front door of her apartment.

"Alice!" her mother called. "If you and Peter are going roller-skating, take Beatrice with you. And remember, only around the block. No crossing streets on skates."

Beatrice appeared, a big smile on her face.

"All right," Alice said and sighed. She glared at Beatrice. "But if you make even one tiny bit of trouble, I'll never take you again."

Beatrice pulled her skates out of the box, too.

"Here we are, Alice." Peter sat down on the edge of the fountain in front of the museum. "Now what?"

"I'm tired," said Beatrice, pulling her skates off her shoulder. "And I'm not walking any more. I want to skate."

"First we have to go inside and investigate," Alice said. "Maybe we'll see the Beard."

Alice dragged Beatrice and Peter up the stone steps leading into the main entrance of the museum.

"You can't come in here with roller skates," the guard at the door said. "You'll have to check them."

"I'm not checking my skates," Peter said. "I'm going home."

Alice knew that tone in Peter's voice. His mind was made up.

"All right, Peter. Let's go over to Madison and back up to Eighty-eighth Street so we can skate."

As they neared Madison Alice stopped. "Peter! Beatrice! Here!" Alice pulled them down behind a row of garbage cans lined up along the curb.

"Not garbage cans again," moaned Peter.

"Shhh!" said Alice. "Look over there!" She pointed to a glassed-in café on the corner.

"So?"

"It's the two suspects," Alice whispered. "They're at the second table on the left. Right next to the glass."

"Hey, that's Miss Slade!" Beatrice shouted.

"Shh! Keep your voice down."

"I don't think they can hear us through the glass, Alice," Peter said.

"You never know. They might have hidden microphones. Notice, Peter, that they are obviously plotting. Look at them. They're leaning over the table."

"I think they're having lunch," Peter said.

"They're slurping their soup," Beatrice added. "I bet it's better than the soup we get at school."

"Peter, anyone can see how suspicious that man is. He has a beard, *and* he's wearing dark glasses."

"My uncle has a beard," Peter reminded Alice. "So did Abraham Lincoln."

"*And* they're looking at pictures," Alice went on. "Probably photos of stolen jewelry."

"Maybe that's her husband," Beatrice suggested. Miss Slade was married, but no one at Miss Barton's had ever seen her husband or even knew her married name.

"Probably photos of their honeymoon," Peter said.

"I think," Alice replied slowly, "that we are on to something very important. I think they may be looking at microfilm. The photos could be a cover for microfilm. Spies always put information on microfilm."

"I thought you said they were stealing jewelry," Peter pointed out. "You said they were suspects in an international ring of jewel thieves."

"That, too. It could be both. Who knows what we've stumbled onto."

At that moment Miss Slade and the man with the beard rose from the table. They left the café arm in arm.

"Quick," Alice said. "Follow me." She raced up the steps of a nearby brownstone for a better view. Peter and Beatrice followed.

"Look," Beatrice said. "He's holding her hand. Kissy, kissy." She puckered her lips.

"Shut up, Beatrice."

"This is nothing but a boring romance," declared Peter. "I'm going home." He slung his skates over his shoulder and trudged off.

"Boys are so unreliable," Alice muttered, wondering

what she would do next. *It might be better to have girls for assistants,* she told herself.

"I want to skate." Beatrice bent over and slid her foot into her skate.

Alice grabbed her. "Look!"

"What?"

"Don't you see, stupid? There's *another* man, and he's following them!" Alice pointed toward Miss Slade and her companion.

They watched a man in a shiny, black, belted raincoat. A black hat was pulled down over his forehead.

"It's not raining, Beatrice. And it is therefore significant that he is wearing a raincoat. I may need you for a witness." Alice gave her sister a determined pinch on the arm.

"Ouch! What's that for?" Beatrice was outraged.

"So you'll *remember.* This is a major clue. And I don't want you to forget it."

That evening Alice was so absorbed in her Apple IIe that her mother had to call her three times before she went in to dinner. After dinner Alice went straight back to the computer and ran her new program.

<u>SUSPECTS</u>
MISS SLADE
THE BEARD
BLACK HAT

Alice stared at the screen for a long time.

CHAPTER FIVE

MONDAY MORNING BLUES

Alice stifled a yawn. It was only 9:30 in the morning, and she was already exhausted. She had been so preoccupied with her discovery of an international ring of jewel thieves that she barely had time to finish her homework the night before. The science assignment had been the worst. She had just started it when her mother told her to go to bed. Alice had made a tent out of her sheet and blankets. She finished the assignment by the light of her pocket flashlight. It wasn't neat, but at least she wouldn't get marked down for being late.

Alice made a mental note to get more batteries. She might need her flashlight again in the very near future. She had to admit that all her work on the Apple IIe hadn't gotten her very far. It was time for a more direct approach. Alice knew that she needed hard evidence. And she would have to be the one to get it. She wouldn't get into the *Guinness Book of World Records* by just *thinking* about great achievements. She had to accomplish something.

Alice vaguely heard Mrs. Parker talking about Columbus and Spanish explorers. Well, it seemed that not only dead people were interested in South American gold! The question was, what did Miss Slade *do* with the gold jewelry after she left the museum?

"Well, Alice? Can you answer the question?" Mrs. Parker stood in front of Alice's desk.

"I bet she hid it."

"You what? Alice, did you hear the question? I asked what Ferdinand and Isabella's reaction was when Columbus returned from his first voyage."

Alice pulled herself together. She realized that she had made an unprofessional blunder. Famous detectives like Hercule Poirot never daydreamed while working on a case. He never let things slip out. He weighed every word he said.

"Excuse me, Mrs. Parker. What I meant to say is that I think Queen Isabella must have hidden her—um—disappointment. I mean that Columbus hadn't discovered China or India."

"Oh. I see. Well, yes. That's possible—at least until Spain began acquiring South American gold." Mrs. Parker returned to the front of the room.

Alice breathed a sigh of relief. At least she wasn't too tired to think. Which reminded her: Where would Miss Slade hide the jewelry? Why not in the art room? Of course! That would explain why she had acted so strangely about Sarah's picture. She wouldn't want anyone snooping around discovering her hiding places. The art room had to be it! Why hadn't she thought of it sooner? Well, there was still time. In fact, lunch period would be perfect for a thorough search. Since Miss Slade always left school and ate lunch at the corner coffee shop, Alice knew the coast would be clear. She could already see the look of surprise and admiration on Peter's face when she confronted him with the evidence. Alice leaned back in her chair and smiled as she imagined how he would apologize for not believing her.

Alice sat in a stall in the bathroom. She had decided to wait there so that she wouldn't have to explain why she wasn't going straight to lunch. In ten minutes she would go to the art room. She wanted to give Miss Slade enough time to leave. She pressed the timer button on her digital watch and set the alarm to go off in ten minutes.

Alice heard a faucet dripping. *Drip, drip, drip.* She tried to imagine what it would feel like to have that same drip landing on your head. That was the Chinese water torture. *Drip, drip, drip.* On your head forever. Well, not forever. Just until you went crazy or confessed.

Alice checked her watch. Nine minutes and twelve seconds to go. It was uncomfortable sitting on the toilet seat. There was nothing to lean against. That would be a pretty good torture—making someone sit on a toilet seat for hours! Not letting them sleep! She remembered hearing that sleep deprivation was one of the most effective tortures known. You didn't have to do a thing. No beatings, electric shocks, burning—just keep the person awake long enough and he would be begging to confess.

Alice checked her watch again. Eight minutes forty-two seconds left. Imagine being in solitary confinement. Alone in a dark prison cell. Day after day. No one to talk to. No books. No Apple IIe. Not even a pencil or pad of paper. The important thing would be to keep up your morale. You would have to be disciplined. It would be hard, but she would do at least one hundred jumping jacks and fifty sit-ups every day. You would have to stay in shape physically and mentally. She'd try to recite all the poems she knew.

"'The boy stood on the burning deck . . .'" How did the rest of that go? She'd try another.

"'O Captain! My Captain! . . .'"

"'Water, water everywhere, Nor any drop to drink . . .'"

Alice decided she'd rather not recite poems about water. They reminded her of the Chinese water torture. Sitting in a dungeon for years would be bad enough without thinking about that.

Maybe she'd make up her own poems and recite them.

Seven minutes and twenty-three seconds. Alice stood up on the toilet seat. She decided to touch her toes a few times to limber up. She was on an upswing with her hands straight above her head when the door to the bathroom opened, and Hilary walked in. Their eyes met.

"What are you doing standing on the toilet with your arms in the air, Alice?"

Alice had had enough. She jumped down and started for the bathroom door. She tried to look as dignified as possible. "I was touching my toes," Alice said as she opened the door and left Hilary behind. Sometimes the truth *was* best.

Miss Slade must have left by then. To make sure, Alice decided to walk up to the seventh floor slowly. At the sixth floor, she checked her watch. Five minutes thirteen seconds. Oh, well, she'd risk it. She opened the stair case door and walked along the maroon- and black-tiled linoleum floor. She hadn't realized before how ugly it was. It really didn't go with the yellow walls.

The art room door was ajar. Alice poked her head inside and called quietly, "Miss Slade?" No answer. She edged into the room. "Oh, Miss Slade?" Still no answer. Good. She closed the door after her. Even if the closed door looked suspicious, it would give her time to hide if she heard anyone coming.

Alice stood in the center of the room, wondering where to start. Her eyes rested on the mannequin. That great white robe could cover a lot of stolen jewelry! Alice went over to the divan. She began to frisk the mannequin, the way the police frisked suspects on TV. It was just a bit harder since the mannequin was lying down. Alice was disappointed. She couldn't feel a single bulge or bump, just hard plastic. Maybe the mannequin was lying on the jewelry. Maybe the divan was hollow. Alice tried to push the mannequin into a sitting position.

Footsteps! Her heart seemed to stop. She pushed the mannequin back down, straightened the jelab as best she could, and hid behind the divan just as the door to the art room opened.

She couldn't see anything, but she knew it was Miss Slade because of the clomps.

"I don't remember shutting the door," Miss Slade mumbled under her breath. "Oh, well, the wind, perhaps. Now where could it be?"

Alice heard Miss Slade clomp over the far side of the room. *Probably heading for her desk,* thought Alice. She heard Miss Slade open a drawer and then shut it. *Clomp, clomp.* Miss Slade walked back toward the door. All of a sudden the alarm on Alice's watch beeped. Before she could turn it off, it beeped again. The clomping stopped. Silence. *Miss Slade must be listening!* Alice thought. She held her breath. She hoped that Miss Slade wouldn't hear her heart pounding.

Clomp, clomp. Miss Slade reached the door. She went out and closed it behind her. Alice relaxed. Then she heard the unmistakable sound of a key turning in the lock.

Alice knew she couldn't panic. A detective was bound to get into tight spots, she thought. That was part of the profession. What made a good detective *great* was coolness in the face of danger. Great detectives always thought best when the danger was the worst. They thrived under the most adverse conditions. Her condition was certainly adverse—or was it? Alice wondered. She might be locked in, but that also meant that everyone else was locked out. The coast really was clear. She would be able to proceed with a full investigation. She would have plenty of time to hide when Miss Slade returned and unlocked the door.

Alice crept out from behind the divan and stood up. She did a few knee bends. Then she turned back to the mannequin. She slipped her hands under the mannequin and felt along the divan. No jewelry. No hollow.

She paused to think. The turban. That must be it! Why else would it be so big? The problem was that she would have to unwind it if she really wanted to do a thorough search, and she wasn't at all sure she would be able to get it back together again. She decided to leave the turban for last. If everything else failed, she'd come back to it. No use tipping off Miss Slade that someone was on to her.

Alice surveyed the room. It was important to be

systematic. She decided to start in one corner and work her way around. She would begin with the kiln. Now that would be a good hiding place! They didn't do pottery at Miss Barton's until after Christmas, so the kiln would be empty. A perfect place to stash jewelry. It even looked like a safe.

Alice turned the kiln handle and swung the heavy doors open. Nothing there.

Alice decided to check the room one last time. Perhaps she had missed something. Often evidence was in the most obvious place. Suddenly her eye was caught by a gleam of sunlight reflecting off the ruby pinned to the mannequin's turban.

"That's it!" she exclaimed aloud. "The jewels are right out in the open. There *is* no hiding place!"

Alice realized that she would need help. Even though Hilary wasn't her favorite person, she *was* a Peach and she knew all about jewelry. Lydia saw all the spy movies and was good at undercover work. And Sarah was Alice's best friend.

Alice looked at her watch. There were only ten minutes to the next class. If she hurried, she could make it to the lunchroom in time to grab a sandwich. Then she remembered. She was locked in! There would be no lunch for Alice Whipple that day. The next period was French, and they were having a quiz. Alice began to feel faint. Low blood sugar! Mr. Moffet, the science teacher, had told them that the best thing they could do before a test was to raise their blood sugar levels.

Alice glanced at the fruit bowl. "No," she said. "Impossible. Ugh!" But she felt another hunger pang. Her feet seemed to move by themselves in the direction of the fruit bowl. "Is this me? Alice Whipple?" she wondered out loud. She knew that desperation made people do all sorts of strange things.

Alice reached out and picked up an apple. There definitely were worm holes. But at least they were only on one side. If she were very careful. If she took only a tiny bite out of the other side. Maybe the worm hadn't wriggled that far. Alice shut her eyes and bit into the apple. She felt something hard. A petrified worm! The fruit *had* been there for ages! Without thinking, she spit it out and heard something bounce on the linoleum. She opened her eyes. She knelt down. It was only the piece of apple she had spit out. Her appetite was gone. And so, she suddenly noticed, was the banana that had been in the fruit bowl for weeks.

Alice replaced the apple in the fruit bowl, bite side down. Then she heard the key turn in the lock. She jumped behind the divan as the door opened. She was glad she had only taken one bite out of the apple. Maybe Miss Slade wouldn't even notice.

Alice rushed into French class. She was six minutes and twenty-two seconds late. Madame de la Meuse, the French teacher, was not pleased. But Alice didn't care, she was just glad to be out of the art room. She had taken a desperate chance. When Miss Slade had clomped out of the room and down the hall, Alice seized the opportunity to escape. She was convinced that she had discovered her true vocation. But the question now was, how was her French?

CHAPTER SIX

LUNCH I

Alice, Sarah, Lydia, and Hilary carried their lunch trays over to a small table for four in the corner of the cafeteria and sat down.

Alice stared at her plate of green salad. She picked up her fork and carefully sifted through the lettuce leaves. She was grateful that she had had friends to call on in her hour of need. Peter had not been helpful at all. Clearly, Alice thought, girls would be better assistants. You couldn't always count on boys. She gently prodded her creamed chicken.

"Well, Alice," Lydia interrupted her musings. "Any bugs in the lunch today?"

"No worms, roaches, or other foreign matter sighted in mine," Alice said. "Nothing in any of yours?" The girls shook their heads. "Must be a Miss Barton's record."

Of course Hilary wasn't worried about finding a bug in her lunch. She had brought hers from home. Sometimes, if you could get a medical excuse about your diet, you were allowed to bring your lunch as long as you ate it in the cafeteria with everyone else.

Alice, Sarah, and Lydia watched Hilary unpack the brown and tan Gucci bag that she used as a lunchbox. She arranged four crackers with pâté and olives in the center of one plate. She surrounded the crackers with a ring of celery sticks filled with English cheddar, her favorite cheese. On another plate Hilary mixed her cold chicken curry with raisins, onions, and almonds. And finally she pulled out a box of McVittie's Digestive Biscuits, which were really only special English crackers. Once she opened the box, she offered the crackers to her friends.

"Now that we are all together," Alice began, "I think it's time to explain why I have called this meeting." She took a long, slow sip of milk.

"Alice," Sarah said. "Why are you whispering?"

"Because, Sarah, this is a secret meeting. And what we have to discuss must not be overheard."

"A secret?" Lydia was thrilled "What kind of a secret?"

"I don't suppose it has anything to do with horses," Hilary said, sounding a bit bored.

"No, Hilary. It has nothing to do with horses. But"— Alice paused—"it *does* have to do with jewelry."

"Oh? What kind of jewelry, Alice?" Hilary patted the pearl necklace under her blouse. "Actually I know quite a lot about jewelry. My mother always takes me with her when she goes to Tiffany's, Cartier or Van Cleef and Arpels."

"That's good, Hilary. In fact, I wanted you to be in on this meeting because of your expertise in jewelry."

Hilary was definitely interested.

"Listen, Alice." Sarah sounded impatient. "Are you going to tell us what this is all about or not?"

"Of course I am," Alice replied. She took a deep breath and launched into her explanation. "You may have noticed that I was not at lunch yesterday and that I was late to French. I sort of thought that you would have noticed, Lydia, since you are so good at spying on people."

Lydia beamed. "I *am* rather good at it, Alice. It's true."

"What about the jewelry, Alice?" Hilary crunched a piece of celery.

"One thing at a time, please. The *reason* I was late to French was that I was locked in the art room. That's where she keeps the stolen jewelry."

"Who keeps what stolen jewelry, Alice?" Hilary asked.

"Miss Slade, of course. That's what this is all about— Miss Slade and stolen jewelry. Now stop interrupting."

Hilary, Lydia, and Sarah waited.

"I was searching the art room for clues," Alice explained. "And I actually found a few. First of all, you remember that old brown banana that Miss Slade kept for still lifes? Well, it's gone. It was there for weeks and now it's gone. I personally find that very suspicious."

"Maybe it's not suspicious, Alice," Sarah said. "Maybe someone got hungry and ate it."

"Exactly!" Alice replied. "It had to be an inside job."

"Inside what?" Lydia asked.

"Inside the school. Just think about it. Only someone at Miss Barton's would know how terrible the lunches are. And only someone who knows how terrible the lunches are would be *desperate* enough to eat that banana."

"I see," Sarah said and paused. "Well, who do you think it was?"

"I don't know," Alice admitted. "That's what makes it a clue. We've got to find out who."

Lydia coughed. She looked guiltily down at her fingernails. "Alice—" she began.

"Yes, Lydia?"

"No one actually ate the banana."

"How do you know?"

"Because I took it."

"You took it?" Alice stared. "What on earth for?"

"Well, it *was* kind of old. And you know Beatrice's friend Emily? Well, she forgot to bring in something moldy for the first grade mold garden they grow every year. She was so upset that she left her moldy cheese at home, she thought the teacher would never forgive her. You know how those babyish first graders worry about doing everything right."

Alice hadn't noticed that Beatrice worried very much. "Lydia," Alice demanded, "are you trying to tell me that you gave that old banana to Emily?"

"Exactly."

"So you see, Alice," Sarah said. "It wasn't a clue after all."

"When are we getting to the jewelry?" Hilary wanted to know.

"All in good time," Alice said. She sipped her milk again, feeling that she needed time to digest the loss of a promising clue.

"Of course there *are* other clues," Alice pointed out.

Sarah, Lydia, and Hilary waited.

"There is the theft from the art room."

"Theft? What theft?" Lydia asked.

"Sarah's unfinished owl picture," Alice declared. "That is certainly an odd development. And, therefore, it is a significant clue."

"Well, it is strange," Lydia admitted. "I don't remember any other pictures disappearing before."

"Who'd want to steal a picture of an old owl anyway?" Hilary asked. "If it were a horse—"

"Ahem." Sarah cleared her throat.

Alice, Lydia, and Hilary looked at Sarah.

There was a strained silence at the table.

"I have something to tell you," Sarah said.

"What is it?" Alice asked. The meeting was not going the way she had planned.

"It's about my owl picture."

"What about it?"

"Well, it didn't actually disappear."

"Then how come it wasn't on the shelf in the art room?"

"I mean—it wasn't really stolen."

"Then where was it?"

"You've got to swear you won't tell if I tell you. I could get in big trouble."

"Listen, Sarah. You've got to tell. Of course we won't tell. Peaches don't tell on each other."

"I took it," Sarah whispered.

"You took it?" Alice was appalled. "Why?"

"Because I wanted to give it to my father for his birthday, and Miss Slade wasn't going to let us take them home in time. So I decided to take it home early and finish it. I pretended it was stolen so Miss Slade wouldn't get angry."

"Sarah, that is the worst thing I ever heard. How could you?"

"Listen, Alice. I don't know why you care. It has nothing to do with you."

"But it was a clue. I wasted a lot of time on it. Detectives don't like getting sidetracked by false leads."

"Detective?" Sarah said. "I thought you were going to be an artist."

"That was before. A lot has happened since then. Now I know that my true vocation is to follow in the footsteps of Sherlock Holmes, Miss Marple, and Hercule Poirot. I am going to be the youngest girl detective in the *Guinness Book of World Records* and I am willing to let you three share my entry as my assistants. There never has been a girl detective, you know."

"What about Nancy Drew?"

"She doesn't count. She's not real."

"What about the Fabulous Five? And the Four Go Adventuring Again?"

"Those are groups, Sarah. I'm talking about a *single* mastermind."

"Oh."

"Well, frankly, Alice, it really doesn't matter," said Hilary. "Because you have no case left. Your clues turned out not to be clues after all."

"That's what you think," Alice retorted.

"You mean there's something else?" Lydia asked hopefully.

"Of course there is." Alice beamed. She had saved the best for last. "The jewels."

"It's about time," Hilary said.

"What jewels?" Sarah sounded distinctly skeptical.

Alice took one last long sip of milk. She turned to Hilary. "It took me quite awhile to realize that the best hiding places are the most obvious ones."

"What hiding places, Alice?" Lydia asked.

"For the jewels."

"What jewels?"

"The stolen jewels. The costume jewelry in the art room obviously is not costume jewelry."

"Then what is it?" Sarah asked.

"It's real, and Miss Slade stole it and hid it in plain sight so no one would get suspicious." Alice leaned back in her chair to let Sarah, Lydia, and Hilary absorb the significance of her discovery.

Hilary drummed her fingers on the table. "Don't be ridiculous, Alice. Anyone can see that the jewelry in the art room is fake. The ruby in the turban doesn't look at all like my mother's ruby ring. And besides, the gold lacqueur is chipping off all the necklaces."

Lydia and Sarah stared at Alice.

Alice was thinking fast. "You may be right, Hilary. But the most important thing is not *where* she hides the jewelry but *how* she steals it."

"Who says she steals it?" Sarah demanded.

"Look, Sarah. Do you remember when we were standing in line in the museum lobby to check our coats?"

"Mmmmmm."

"And do you remember when Miss Slade went up to the information desk and met a man?"

"So what? I bet it was her husband." Sarah pushed her plate across the table and munched on one of Hilary's biscuits.

Alice ignored Sarah's remark. It reminded her of Peter's attitude.

"And do you remember his beard? And his dark glasses?"

"So?"

"So I think that clinches it."

"Clinches what?"

"That they are both up to no good."

"What are you talking about, Alice?"

"Look, Sarah. Don't you remember that he handed her a brown paper bag?"

"It was probably a sandwich. She never eats lunch at school."

"Sarah, if you're not going to be serious, I won't tell you the next thing."

"Okay, Alice."

"*And* Miss Slade put the paper bag in her handbag."

"So?"

"So. And do you remember when I left the exhibit?"

"Yes?"

"Well. When I went to the ladies' room, I really didn't intend to go to the ladies' room. I just said I was going there because I wanted to follow Miss Slade."

"What happened?" Lydia sounded interested again.

"I lost her." Alice chewed slowly on a biscuit.

"What do you mean? Weren't you following her?"

Yes, Lydia. I was. But this group of tourists came between us. By the time I got around them, Miss Slade had disappeared. I decided to check the cafeteria. Then I went to the ladies' room. As I was standing in the ladies' room—"

"But I thought you said you didn't really go to the ladies' room," Hilary pointed out.

"If you all keep interrupting, I'll never finish explaining."

"Okay, so you were standing in line in the ladies' room—"

"And Miss Slade came in. Luckily I was behind a fat lady so Miss Slade didn't see me. She went up to the mirror, took the paper bag from her handbag, opened it, and took out a gold necklace."

"A gold necklace?" Hilary asked.

"Are you *sure* it was gold?"

"See, I told you, Alice," Sarah said. "That man was her husband."

"Look, Sarah, do husbands wear dark glasses and give their wives gold necklaces in brown paper bags by the information desk at the Metropolitan Museum of Art? Please be serious."

"Well. Maybe he's her boyfriend." Sarah giggled.

"Sarah! Boyfriends may wear dark glasses. And they may stand by the information desk at the Metropolitan Museum of Art. But do they give presents to their girlfriends in brown paper bags?"

"Maybe it was a gift he just bought at the shop," Sarah suggested. "A copy of a gold necklace."

"Then it would have been in a museum bag, right," Alice said triumphantly.

"I—I guess so." Sarah studied the crumbs from her biscuit.

"May I continue?" Alice was in her stride. She imagined herself in a courtroom, defending an innocent client wrongly charged with murder. Maybe she would go to law school.

"What happened next, Alice?"

"Miss Slade put on the gold necklace."

"Oh." Sarah sounded disappointed.

"And it had emeralds on it."

"Emeralds?" Hilary asked. "How many emeralds?"

"A lot," said Alice. "And then she tied her shawl around her shoulders."

"So what?"

"She was obviously hiding the necklace."

"And?"

"We all left the museum."

"That's true. Is that all?"

"No, Sarah. That's not all. Miss Slade got the necklace out of the museum by *wearing* it. It had to be stolen."

"How can you be sure it wasn't a present, Alice?"

"Don't you understand the connections?" Alice could see that Sarah didn't. "Class trips are a perfect cover for meetings at the museum if she wants to smuggle stolen jewelry out of the museum in question. I think it's an open-and-shut case, don't you?"

"But what does it all mean?"

"That's not the point, Sarah. The point is that we are on to something big! We can figure out the details later. What we need now is Imagination not Technique!" Alice paused. "Tomorrow we'll start drawing up lists. I think we've discovered enough for one day."

Alice was relieved that the biggest clue still held the interest of her companions.

They agreed to meet again the following day.

Then Miss Slade entered the cafeteria.

Alice, Sarah, Lydia, and Hilary stared.

Miss Slade was wearing the exact same gold necklace that the girls had been discussing.

Mr. Moffet, the science teacher, passed Miss Slade on his way out of the cafeteria. "Why, Sally," he said. "What a stunning necklace!"

"Thank you, Jason." Sally Slade smiled. "Do you really

like it? My husband brought it back from his last field trip to South America. Emeralds are so much less expensive down there."

"Well, it's lovely. I'll see you later at the faculty meeting."

Sarah, Lydia, and Hilary glared at Alice.

"I think you should go back to being an artist," Sarah said, rising from the table.

"Maybe you could learn to like horseback riding," Hilary suggested. "Women can be quite good jockeys."

"Actually," Lydia said, "your owl isn't bad now that it's painted in. I agree with Sarah. You really could be an artist."

Alice said nothing. Sometimes, she thought, silence was the best policy.

CHAPTER SEVEN

A NEW SUSPECT

The final bell rang on Thursday. Alice had been very discouraged the past two days with the results of her first case.

Miss Barton's students were pouring out of the school building. Alice could instantly spot the fifth-graders because that day was the day they were taking home their owl pictures. Even though Alice found hers difficult to carry, she had to admit that it was impressive.

Alice wondered where Beatrice was. They were supposed to meet in front of the school bus, but Beatrice wasn't there. Alice scanned the crowd of girls and finally saw Beatrice.

Mrs. Barton's was located at the end of East Eighty-first Street and overlooked the East River. Beatrice was standing by a protective railing. She was talking to a man who looked vaguely familiar to Alice. He wasn't a teacher, she knew. Maybe he was a parent.

But Beatrice knew she was not allowed to talk to strangers. Alice edged her way through the crowd of girls.

She had to turn from side to side so that her owl picture would not be squashed.

"Come on, Beatrice. We'll miss the bus." Alice grabbed Beatrice by the arm and yanked her away.

"What did you pull my arm so hard for, Alice? Do you want me to remember something?"

"Who was that, Beatrice?"

"A nice man."

"What do you mean 'a nice man'? Haven't you been told not to talk to strangers? He might have wanted to kidnap you. He might have tortured you with the Chinese water torture. Or thrown you into a dark, moldy dungeon and made you eat wormy apples and rotten bananas!"

Beatrice began to cry.

"Shut up, Beatrice! What did he want?"

"He was a nice man," wailed Beatrice. "He was asking about owls."

"Well, what did he want to know? And why did he ask you? You don't have an owl."

"But I do, too, have an owl. Every class has an owl, stupid. And the first grade owl is the best."

"What did he want to know, Beatrice?" Alice was beginning to feel exasperated. Hercule Poirot did not have to interrogate people like Beatrice.

"I'm not telling."

"Do you want Mommy and Daddy to know that you were talking to a strange man? They'll really punish you. No dinner. You won't be able to watch reruns of 'Little House on the Prairie'—"

Beatrice started to cry again.

"Look, Beatrice. Just tell me what he wanted."

"He wanted to know about the owl," Beatrice said, sniffling.

Alice decided to try a new tack. She was getting nowhere fast. "What did you tell him, Beatrice?"

"I told him about our mascot."

Alice gave up. She saw Sarah out of the corner of her eye. Sarah was the only fifth-grader without an owl. Alice was too tired to think about owls anymore. In fact, she didn't want to think about owls or jewelry ever again.

That evening Alice was at her desk typing a list into her computer. She had started a new file, Things Detectives Should Not Do. Alice realized that her first case was closed. But she was determined to be prepared for the next.

"Finished your homework, Alice?" Mr. Whipple asked as he walked into her room. He thought Alice had been neglecting her homework lately.

"Almost, Daddy. I was taking a little break."

Mr. Whipple peered over Alice's shoulder. "Why are 'watch beepers' a problem, Alice?"

"Oh, it's nothing. Just a new thing I'm trying to program." Alice pressed the Save button and turned off her computer.

Alice awoke with a start. It was the middle of the night. She sat up. Her mind was churning. Things were even more complicated than she had imagined! She suddenly realized why the man talking to Beatrice the other day had looked familiar. He was the same man who had followed Miss Slade and the Beard. The Man in the Black Hat and

Raincoat! And furthermore he was the same man she had seen staring at Miss Slade in the museum. Only that time he was holding his hat and coat. Something *was* going on after all. But whahing *was* going on
after all. But what?

CHAPTER EIGHT

BREAK-IN AT MISS BARTON'S

On Friday, even before the Miss Barton's school bus pulled up on Eighty-first Street and East End Avenue, Alice and Beatrice sensed excitement in the air.

"Hey! Look!" Beatrice nudged Alice. "Police! All over the place!"

"Quiet, Beatrice! I'm thinking." Alice stared at the cul-de-sac, which ran from East End Avenue to the river. Police barricades were blocking traffic and crowds of onlookers milled about. Alice noticed that some curtains and blinds were slightly opened in the building across the street from the school. Faces peered out at the commotion. Alice knew it was too early for a fire drill because no one was in school yet.

"I bet it's a bomb scare!" Beatrice declared as she and Alice got off the bus.

There *had* been bomb scares at Miss Barton's.

Alice decided to find out what was going on. Halfway down the block, Alice approached a young policeman. He was trying to keep a space open in the crowd so the girls and teachers could get to the school building.

"Excuse me, officer, sir—" Alice began.

"Is there a murder?" Beatrice was more direct than Alice. "I bet there's a corpse."

"No, of course not," the policeman said and smiled. "There was a break-in at the school, and someone's been arrested."

"Oh." Alice was worried. It was just as she had feared. There had been a case, after all. And someone *else* had solved it. Alice had to try to find out what was going on.

"Does this have anything to do with the man who talked to Beatrice?" she asked the officer.

"The man who talked to Beatrice?" He looked puzzled.

Standard interrogation procedure, Alice thought to herself. *If you answer a question with a question, you don't give away anything.*

She would try again.

"You know, the one who follows people?"

"Follows people?"

Obviously a well-trained policeman, Alice thought. But then he didn't have anything else to do. It would be difficult for her to get her training to be a good detective and still do all of her homework, too. Miss Barton's gave you a lot of homework. Still, Alice told herself, there was no excuse. All great detectives learned to work under pressure. Now that she had blown her case, Alice was considering the magnitude of her defeat. There would be no *Guinness Book of World Records* for Alice Whipple now.

She entered the school building. It was a lot less crowded than the street.

Alice noticed that Miss Carlyle was standing outside her office, talking to a police officer. Miss Carlyle was director of admissions at Miss Barton's. She was thin and had curly white hair. Alice had never seen Miss Carlyle bend over. She reminded Alice of a ruler, with arms and legs and a head. Miss Carlyle had taught posture at Miss Barton's before she became admissions director.

As soon as the policeman sauntered off, Alice edged toward Miss Carlyle.

"Good morning, Miss Carlyle. Why are there so many policemen? Did anything happen?"

"Hey!" Beatrice interrupted. "Look, Alice!"

Alice turned and saw a man being led toward the side door by two policemen. He was handcuffed. It was Black Hat!

"As you can see, Alice," Miss Carlyle said, "something *has* happened." Miss Carlyle bent her elbow to look at her watch. Her forearm was at a right angle to her upper arm. "There will be an assembly first period, and Mrs. Partridge will inform the student body and the faculty of what has happened. You had better hurry now or you'll be late for homeroom."

Alice pulled Beatrice aside. "Just exactly what did you say to that man yesterday, Beatrice?"

"I already told you. He kept asking about owls. So I told him about our mascot."

Alice knew that there was still an unsolved mystery. It had something to do with Black Hat and owls, not Miss Slade and jewelry.

"Listen, Alice. If there's going to be an assembly, maybe I should tell about talking to that man yesterday," Beatrice said.

"Don't you dare!"

"Well, why not? I could get up on stage and make a big announcement. I'd be a star. After all, I *am* the one he spoke to. Maybe they'd turn a spotlight on me and—"

"Beatrice, if you dare say a single word I won't let you be my assistant. Don't you want your name in the *Guinness Book of World Records* as the youngest female assistant in the whole world?"

Alice was pleased with the new development. The case had been reopened.

"Wel-l-l—"

"Beatrice, if you ruin this case, I will make steak out of Salisbury."

Salisbury was Beatrice's pet turtle.

"You can't do that, Alice. You'd get in such big trouble—"

"And I wouldn't let you be in the *Guinness Book of World Records* with me, either."

"You'll have to buy Salisbury a new decoration for his tank. For saying such mean things about him."

At assembly, Mrs. Partridge explained that an unidentified man had broken into the school during the early morning hours. For some unknown reason, he went into the first grade classroom. The cleaning staff had mopped the floor just before he entered. It was apparently still wet because the intruder had slipped and fallen. He was lying dazed on the floor when he was discovered by the cleaning staff. No one understood why he was clutching the first grade mascot. Mrs. Partridge said that perhaps he had psychological problems. She reassured the students that there was nothing further to worry about. The police would take care of everything.

Alice had heard enough. She detected signs of a cover-up. She would have to talk to Sarah, Lydia, and Hilary. Her suspicions had been right all along. Only the clues and the suspects were different.

CHAPTER NINE

LUNCH II

"Okay, Alice, what's up?" Sarah put her tray down and sat next to Alice at a corner table in the school cafeteria.

"If you don't mind, Sarah, I'll wait for Hilary and Lydia before I explain."

"Uh, oh! You haven't discovered another plot, have you, Alice?" Sarah had begun the delicate task of investigating each layer of her lasagna and checking its contents.

"I got here as soon as I could." Lydia slammed down her lunch tray and breathlessly slid into the seat opposite Alice. "I wanted to make sure I wasn't being followed, so I had to double back through the lunch line."

"For goodness sake, Lydia, everyone can see that you're sitting here. It's hardly top secret!" Sarah's eyes were glued to her lasagna. Alice sensed that Sarah was in no mood to hear about a new plot. She would be hard to convince. Alice would have to choose her words carefully.

"Sorry I'm a bit late, Alice." Hilary put down her Gucci

bag and began unpacking small, plastic containers from Zabar's, a well-known New York gourmet food shop.

"I'm sorry, Hilary, but there's no time for that."

"Not time for what, Alice? Hey, who'd like a smoked mussel?" Hilary held out one of the opened containers.

"That's just what I'd like to know," said Sarah. "They smell disgusting."

"The English love them."

"They would!" Sarah took a large bite of her lasagna.

"Look, everyone, something important has come up. Something that will require immediate attention. We'll need to use lunchtime for investigating, not eating!"

"But, Alice, today I have smoked salmon as well as smoked mussels," Hilary said, almost wailing. "Look, Alice," Hilary said. "I don't want to hear another word about Miss Slade or about jewelry! Can't we just enjoy our lunch and talk?"

"Maybe you can enjoy your lunch, Hilary, but it's hard for the rest of us, who have to be on constant guard against foreign matter!"

Sarah's lasagna hadn't improved her mood, Alice thought. Obviously Sarah didn't want to hear another word about mysteries. "Hilary," Alice said, "this has nothing to do with Miss Slade or with jewelry. It has—"

"Does that mean that I'm going to get to do some spying?" Lydia asked between bites of her ham and cheese sandwich. "If so, I'll need all my strength." Lydia took a huge gulp of milk.

"Calm down, Lydia." Alice was relieved that at least one person at the table appeared interested in what she was saying.

"Okay, what's up, Alice? Why don't you just tell us?"

"I've been trying to, Sarah. Look, I know that all the stuff about Miss Slade and the jewelry was a wild goose chase. But something really is happening in this school. Why else would a man break in?"

"But, Alice, Mrs. Partridge has already explained all that."

"Come on, Hilary. Mrs. Partridge's speech was obviously a cover-up!"

"It was?" Hilary placed a small piece of smoked salmon on a Carr's water biscuit and ate it.

"Oh, great, I love cover-ups!" Lydia dropped her half-eaten sandwich and stared at Alice.

"Alice, just tell us what you're talking about." Sarah was beginning to sound really annoyed.

"I have some information about the man they caught."

"What kind of information?" The excitement in Lydia's voice was unmistakable.

"The break-in had nothing to do with psychological problems."

"How do you know that, Alice?" Sarah asked.

Was Alice imagining things, or did Sarah sound just a little bit interested? "Because Beatrice told me."

"Come off it, Alice!"

No, Sarah did not sound interested. "This time Beatrice is a good source," Alice protested.

"Look, Alice. The man was found clutching the first grade mascot in his arms! Does that sound like a perfectly sane and reasonable man, or what?"

"Sarah, things are seldom what they seem."

"What is that supposed to mean?"

"What it means, Sarah, is that I know for a fact that the break-in had nothing to do with psychological problems. The man was definitely after owls."

"How do you know that?"

"Because the man who was arrested asked Beatrice about owls."

"He did?" Sarah actually looked up at Alice from her plate. "Why did he ask about owls?"

"That's exactly what we're going to find out!" Alice relaxed. It just took putting things the right way and then people would listen to you.

"But, Alice, what owls?" Lydia sounded perplexed. "The school is filled with owls." Lydia paused for a moment and rolled her eyes to the ceiling. "There are thirteen stuffed owl mascots. One for each grade, plus kindergarten. Every student at Miss Barton's owns a blazer with an owl emblem on the pocket. We all take gym and wear gym shorts, and each pair of shorts has an owl on it. Let's assume that each girl has three pairs of gym shorts. According to last year's year book, there are six hundred and forty-three girls enrolled at Miss Barton's." Lydia whipped out the calculator from her uniform pocket. "That makes one thousand nine hundred and twenty-nine pairs of gym shorts and six hundred and forty-three blazers. But that's not all! Since the school started its fund-raising campaign, owls are positively everywhere!"

"She's right." Hilary swallowed the last bit of her smoked salmon. "My mother's head of the fund-raising committee and they've put owls on everything to raise money. Owls are on T-shirts, nightshirts, sweatshirts, hats, scarves, umbrellas, knapsacks, year books, the school magazine, school coloring books—you can even buy owl Kleenex!"

"And, of course, there's the Miss Barton's owl on the school banner in the assembly hall," Sarah interjected.

"Yes," said Hilary. "I've always liked that banner. It's made out of silk, you know. Just the sort of thing medieval English knights rode into battle with."

"A banner with an owl? Be serious, Hilary!"

Alice realized she was losing control. If she didn't say something right then and there, Sarah and Hilary would start fighting about the English. That was the last thing Alice wanted. There was too much at stake. But how could she convince Sarah and Hilary and Lydia to do what she knew had to be done?

Alice tapped her milk glass with her fork. She knew adults tapped their water glasses when they gave speeches at parties. "Ahem!"

"Is there something the matter with your voice, Alice?"

"No, Lydia, I am calling for attention."

Hilary leaped up from her seat and saluted.

"Not that kind of attention, Hilary. All I mean is that I want each and every one of you to pay attention and listen to what I have to say."

"Alice, I think I've had enough. First you say I can't eat. Then you tell me I can't salute. During the entire time I've had the privilege of being a Peach I have tried to live up to the ideals of Peachdom. I have offered my services to you whenever possible. I have supported you. I have been,"— Hilary paused for effect—"or, rather, I have tried to be, a loyal Peach and a loyal friend."

You had to give it to Hilary, Alice thought as she

watched Hilary carefully seal the tops of the plastic containers of food and replace them in her Gucci bag. She really could deliver a speech. Alice knew that Hilary watched videos of all the old movies and that she was trying to memorize Ashley Wilkes's part from *Gone With The Wind*. According to Hilary, Ashley sounded like a real Englishman. Alice preferred Rhett Butler. But that was a matter of taste, and detectives were after facts, not taste.

"We are all clearly under stress," Alice said, looking directly at Hilary.

"We are? Who says?" Sarah asked.

Alice decided to ignore Sarah for the moment. "Yes, we are all under stress. And if I have offended anyone," Alice said, looking directly at Hilary, "I am very sorry. I need all the help I can get. The assembly was a sham. Mrs. Partridge is hiding something, and all of us know it, whether we want to believe it or not."

"It was? We do?" Lydia asked.

"Yes, Lydia. We do. Just think, why would an adult go into the first grade homeroom? And why would an adult fall down clutching the first grade owl mascot? But most important of all, why would an adult talk to Beatrice?"

"That's right, Alice! Why did that man talk to Beatrice? What did she tell him?"

"I told you, Sarah, she told him about an owl. But she didn't talk to him about any old owl, so we don't have to worry about all the owls Lydia mentioned. Beatrice only told him about the owl mascot in her first grade home-room. That's why he went there. Only he didn't know how many other owl mascots there were at Miss Barton's! He must have got the wrong one. Don't you see?"

"I do see." Lydia fell back dramatically in her chair. "It has to be an international owl plot."

"Okay, Lydia, enough of the spy stuff. Let's hear what Alice has to say."

Good old Sarah, thought Alice. When you needed her, she always came through. "Thanks, Sarah. As I was saying, a grown-up man wouldn't talk to someone like Beatrice and then break into a school because of what she'd said unless that man already knew something—something about owls. And then he tried to get information out of Beatrice. The problem was he didn't know whom he was dealing with!"

"You can say that again!" Sarah was actually smiling.

"The question is"—Alice decided to pause for effect—"why was he after owls?"

"For the microfilm," Lydia said.

"For what, Lydia?" Alice was thinking hard.

"For the microfilm hidden inside."

"What microfilm?"

"Look, Alice, what you thought was a ring of jewel thieves is obviously a spy ring. Don't you see? And spies use microfilm."

"It could also be a drug ring. I've seen movies where they hide drugs in stuffed animals." Hilary had stopped packing the containers into her Gucci bag.

"Look, we don't know what he was after. That's the point. We have to find out."

"How, Alice? How can we find out?" Sarah looked really concerned.

"We have to find out if anything is hidden in one of the owls."

"How can we do that without cutting them open? Oh! Blood and gore!"

"For goodness sake, Lydia, they're only stuffed animals!"

"Sarah's right, Lydia. They're stuffed animals and stuffed animals are usually filled with kapok. What we have to do is determine if the kapok is evenly distributed."

"What you really mean, Alice, is that you want us to go around pinching all the owl mascots in Miss Barton's! Isn't that it?"

Alice had to admit that Sarah often had a way of getting right to the point. "Well, in a manner of speaking, yes."

"But if it's microfilm, it will crinkle and be ruined."

"But at least we will have found it, Lydia."

"How do you suggest we go around pinching mascots, Alice? I mean, what will people say?"

"That's precisely why I said lunch would be short. This is the perfect time to visit all the homerooms. Everyone is here and no one is there. Well, at least I hope no one will be there."

"Then we'd better get organized. Right, Alice?"

"Right, Lydia."

"And that's my department? Right, Alice?"

"Right, Lydia."

"Okay. Let's start by synchronizing our watches." Lydia looked at her Timex. "It is precisely 12:02. Got it, everyone? Good. In exactly two minutes we will start. That will make it 12:04, which means we will have twenty-six minutes until the bell for the next class. There are four of us and twelve mascots to investigate. We don't have to bother about the first grade mascot because the man obviously didn't find what he wanted in it. If we allow seven minutes per mascot, which should be plenty of time, that means that we will have five minutes in which to get back and report to Alice. For extra security, I advise that we do not meet in our homeroom but down the hall in front of the third floor broom closet. Does that sound good to you, Alice?"

"Very good, Lydia. There's only one thing left to do, assign the homerooms. Hilary, you take the ones on the second floor and Lydia the ones on the third floor. Sarah, you take the fourth floor. And I'll take the fifth." Alice stood up. "Till we meet at the broom closet! And good luck!"

"Lydia, what are you doing with the third grade mascot?"

"I wanted to see—to see—to see if—"

"To see what, Lydia? Speak up. I can't hear you."

"To see the label, Miss Chestnut."

"Whatever for, Lydia?"

"We're—we're conducting a survey, Miss Chestnut, to see if the mascots are—safe. I mean water—no—fireproof! Thank you, Miss Chestnut. You'll be glad to know this one is just fine!"

Before Miss Chestnut could say another word, Lydia had disappeared.

What a stupid place to put it! Sarah thought as she balanced on the chair with the broom in her hand and tried to nudge the sixth grade mascot from the top shelf of the bookcase. "I'll never get it back up there!" The mascot toppled to the floor. Sarah jumped down and began to squeeze it.

* * *

"I am not stealing your mascot, Brenda Higgins!" Hilary stared down at the freckled face of the irate second-grader.

"Oh, yes, you are, and I'm going to tell!"

"Brenda, have you ever tasted Polo Mints? They're English. A bit like Lifesavers, only much better. If you'd like, I could let you have a roll, but first—"

"Alice Whipple, why are you squeezing that mascot?"

"What, me, Miss Sargent?"

"Yes, you, Alice."

"It's for—it's a—we're—I mean I—"

"Yes, Alice?"

"It's a dust test, Miss Sargent. That's it. A dust test! You see, we're squeezing all the mascots to see if they make us sneeze. The dust, you know." Alice wasn't sure Miss Sargent did know, but she didn't want to wait to find out.

"It was humiliating, Alice!" Sarah leaned against the door to the broom closet, her arms folded across her chest. "What would you have said if someone had found you pinching a mascot with a broom in your hand? And there were positively no lumps in it, and nothing crinkled, either!"

"Alice, your crazy ideas are getting expensive. This one cost me two packs of Polos. And I didn't find a thing."

"Neither did I, Alice. I had to make up some dumb story about checking the mascots for safety."

Before Alice had time to say anything, the bell for class rang. One more dead end. From the looks on her friends' faces, Alice knew she had lost her credibility once again.

CHAPTER TEN

BRAINSTORM

Alice sat glumly in front of the television set on Sunday afternoon. She was watching *The Maltese Falcon* on the VCR. She was too depressed to go with Beatrice to James's birthday party. Her career as a detective seemed to be over.

Sydney Greenstreet was explaining the history of the Maltese Falcon to Humphrey Bogart. The golden bird had been stolen from the Knights of Malta during the Crusades. The thieves had disguised it under a thick coat of black paint.

Alice sat up. "That explains it!" she cried aloud.

She pressed the pause button on the VCR remote control and rushed to the telephone.

"Listen, Peter. Something very exciting has happened."

"Now what, Alice? I'm in the middle of James's party."

"Well, this is more important."

"It can't be that important."

"Yes, it can. If you come over right now, I'll teach you how to write a computer program."

"You will?"

"Of course I will. I'll show you how I program my list of suspects. It's changed, you know. There's been an arrest. A lot of things have happened."

"What kind of things? And who's been arrested?"

"An important suspect. With policemen and everything. At school. There were police all over the streets and inside the front hall. I saw them taking away the suspect myself."

"But it's Sunday, Alice."

"I know it's Sunday, Peter. The arrest was on Friday. It takes time to solve a difficult case."

"Okay, Alice. I'll be right over."

"Look at this, Peter." Alice was eagerly typing on her computer keyboard. "This is my suspect program."

```
LAST PROGRAM
110 PRINT SUSPECTS
120 INPUT A
130 LET A-BLACK HAT
140 PRINT A
150 END
```

"What are those numbers for?" Peter wanted to know.

"This language is called BASIC. You have to program a computer in a language."

"Does it help with French?"

"No, but my father says when I get to Latin in seventh grade that it will help with computers."

"Oh." Peter wasn't sure he saw the connection.

"And the numbers give you the order of the information," Alice explained. "You put in a storage space identified by a capital letter and give it a name. That's called "input." Then you tell the computer to print the letter, and it prints what the letter equals. When you're finished, you write *End*. Is that clear, Peter?"

"Sort of. But what exactly is the point?"

"So you can run the program, of course."

"I'd like to see you run the program."

Alice typed *Run* and

SUSPECTS
BLACK HAT

appeared on the screen.

"Is that all?" Peter asked. "It seems like an awful lot of fuss just to list one thing."

"What's that supposed to mean? That's the list of suspects. That's the program. It's only your first lesson, Peter. I'm trying to make it simple."

"Why couldn't you just make a list with a pencil and a piece of paper?" Peter thought maybe his parents were right about computers after all. "And who is Black Hat? He wasn't on your other list."

"Peter, that is very observant of you. Obviously you have an eye for detail. Every detective needs an eye for detail. Black Hat is my code name for the man arrested at school. He's also the man Beatrice and I saw following Miss Slade and the Beard after you deserted us outside that restaurant."

"Really? You wouldn't think people would be arrested at a school like Miss Barton's."

"Yes," Alice went on. "They were taking him away just as I got to school. Everyone in the neighborhood was watching. In fact, I thought maybe my case was blown but luckily—"

"Your case?" Peter interrupted.

"Exactly. It's why I wanted to see you today, Peter."

"Oh?"

"Yes. You see, we have to get into the school ourselves."

"We? Who's we?"

"You and me, Peter. I've given this a lot of thought, and there is only one thing for us to do."

"Alice, I haven't the slightest idea what you're talking about."

"We're going to sneak into Miss Barton's and search the art room."

"Oh, no, we're not. You said they arrested a man for that. I'm going home."

"He was arrested for breaking in, not sneaking in. We are going to sneak in."

"We are? Why?"

"Look at my list of clues, Peter." Alice typed *Run Clues* and pressed Enter.

Peter saw

CLUES

OWL

BREAK-IN

MALTESE FALCON

on the computer screen.

"What is all that?" Peter asked.

"Those are my new clues. They tell us that there is a fabulously valuable gold owl in Miss Barton's art room and that it has been painted as a disguise. Black Hat must be the thief who stole the golden owl from the exhibit at the Metropolitan Museum. Mrs. Parker told us about the theft during our class trip. I bet Black Hat hid the real one in the gift shop at the museum until he could get it out."

"But how did he get it to Miss Barton's?"

Alice beamed. "I just figured that out. It's just like the Maltese Falcon. Miss Slade bought reproductions of the owls for the art room. She must have bought the real one that he had hidden in the gift shop. It's perfect."

"But how did he do it, Alice?"

"Listen, Peter, I haven't worked out all the details. But if he hadn't substituted the owl and it isn't in Miss Barton's art room right now, then why did he stare at Miss Slade in the museum? Why did he follow Miss Slade and the Beard? Why did he ask Beatrice about owls? Why did he break into Miss Barton's? And why was he caught with an owl? It's perfectly clear that he was after an owl, but he got the wrong one, thanks to Beatrice. I think that clinches it. My only mistake was getting sidetracked by the jewelry. I thought Miss Slade was stealing jewelry from the museum. But now I realize that Black Hat was after the golden owl. He was just using Miss Slade."

"Alice, I think you should tell the police and let them find the owl."

"But I don't have all the proof yet, Peter. Miss Marple, Hercule Poirot, and Sherlock Holmes never discuss their cases with the police until they have all the proof and have solved the case. Besides—" Alice paused.

"Yes?"

"It is my intention, Peter, to become the youngest female detective in history. And—"

"Yes-s-s-s?"

"I might let you share my entry in the *Guinness Book of World Records.*"

"Well."

Alice could tell that Peter was almost convinced.

"You'd think," he continued, "that if it were real gold, other people would be after it, too."

It was clear to Alice that Peter had not seen *The Maltese Falcon.* "That's just the point, Peter. A lot of different people were after the Maltese Falcon, too. That's why we have to get into the school and find the right owl. And we have to do it tomorrow right after school. And we're going to need equipment because we might be there a while."

"What kind of equipment?"

"Flashlight, pocketknife, rope, and food. We'll need sandwiches and a thermos filled with water."

"Sandwiches? Why sandwiches?"

"Well, we might miss dinner."

"I'm not allowed to miss dinner."

"Tell your parents you're having dinner with me. I'll tell mine that I'm having dinner with you. We'll be back long before bedtime."

"I'd rather have milk than water."

"Milk curdles."

"Okay, I'll bring the water. You bring the sandwiches."

"We'll also need some fruit for natural sugar. Raisins. I'll bring raisins. You bring apples. Peter, you'd better make a list. You might forget something."

"Why do we need a rope?"

"Just in case. We've got to be prepared. Maybe I'll bring a nutpick from my grandmother's set, just in case we need to scratch paint off some of the owls."

"What's a nutpick?"

"It's a little instrument for picking walnuts out of the shell."

Alice paused. She stared at Peter.

"What is it, Alice?"

"Miss Barton's is a girls' school," Alice pointed out. "And you're a boy. You'll need a disguise." Alice knew that Peter had been the star of his school play the previous year and that he loved costumes.

"Great! I could dress up as the Con Ed man. Or an electrician. Or a repair man."

"Those are workmen. They use the side entrance. I'd want you to come in the front entrance with me."

"I know! An exterminator! Exterminators have to go through every room in the building. Besides, Miss Barton's is right on the East River. I bet it's full of rats and mice. You can get the plague from rats. There was a lot of plague in the Middle Ages."

"There are no mice and no rats at Miss Barton's," Alice insisted. "Only cockroaches. They get into the salad."

"Well, you need an exterminator for cockroaches."

"Peter, I have a much better costume planned for you. One that will require all your acting abilities. But you're not quite ready for it yet."

"I'm not?"

"No. First we have to do something with your hair."

"Sherlock Holmes never cared what people thought about him," Alice said.

"But Alice," Peter protested. "Sherlock Holmes never had to do this."

"Think of Miss Marple. She didn't care what people said about her."

"Miss Marple was old, Alice."

"Very well, Peter, hand over your wardrobe. If the challenge is too much for you, I entirely understand. I will find someone else to share my entry in the *Guinness Book of World Records*. After all, detectives are born, not made. No amount of persuading can make a person daring, enterprising, resourceful—"

"Okay, Alice," Peter said and sighed. "But you better promise not to tell anyone about this. If the kids at school ever find out—"

"Alice! Alice!"

Before Alice could get to her door, Beatrice tumbled into the room.

"Get out, Beatrice! You are not allowed in my room."

"Alice, why is Peter in his underwear?"

"Look, Beatrice, Peter and I are very busy right now and we don't want to be disturbed."

"And what have you done with Peter's hair? I'm going to tell."

"That's enough, Beatrice." Alice pushed her sister toward the door.

"I won't go. And you can't make me!" Beatrice ducked under Alice's arm and dove under her desk. "I bet you're playing doctor, and I'm going to watch—"

"No, we're not! And you are going to get out now!"

"If you don't let me watch, I promise I will tell Mommy and Daddy what you're doing."

"Beatrice, have you ever tasted Polo Mints?"

CHAPTER ELEVEN

SNEAK-IN AT MISS BARTON'S

Alice had carefully mapped out every detail of her plan. Peter's school ended at 3:00 PM, giving him plenty of time to arrange his disguise and meet Alice at Miss Barton's. By 4:30 PM most of the girls and teachers were preparing to go home. So, at precisely 4:32 PM, Alice wrote her name on the sign-out sheet in the front hall and said goodbye to Miss Rathbone at the switchboard.

Beatrice had already left school for a dentist appointment, so Alice didn't have to explain her absence from the school bus. Alice left the building and turned toward the East River. Right by the railing separating the cul-de-sac from the river were five large garbage cans and several black plastic garbage bags. Alice rapped three times on the metal cans. That was the signal. Peter stood up. He was wearing one of Alice's uniforms and a curly blond wig that was slightly lopsided.

"It's about time, Alice. It really smells back here. Do you think Miss Barton's has this much garbage every day?" Peter wrinkled his nose a few times, trying to air it out.

"You look excellent, Peter. Except push the wig back a bit." Alice nodded with approval. "Do you have everything in your knapsack?"

"Yes. But I've had a lot of trouble with this uniform. It doesn't fit right." Peter squirmed his shoulders uncomfortably.

"Come on, Peter. Everyone's leaving. We've got to get back inside without anyone getting suspicious. Timing is essential in an operation like this one."

Alice and Peter waited to enter the school building until a group of late students was going out. Miss Rathbone looked up for a moment but she was so busy answering phone calls that she barely noticed Alice and her friend.

"Just going back for a book I forgot," Alice said quickly.

Once inside, Peter focused on his discomfort again. "This uniform is too long, Alice. You said it would be a perfect fit."

"Well, I am a bit taller than you. What do you expect? Besides, it's better this way. The skirt covers more of your legs."

"And the socks keep falling down. You must have fat calves."

"Well, pull them up, Peter. You've got boy's legs. And my calves are not fat. They're shapely. Yours are straight up and down, like sticks."

"Listen, Alice, don't be rude after all the sacrifices I've made. It seems to me that things would be simpler if you wore *normal* clothes to school," Peter added, fidgeting once more. "I left the gym shorts home, by the way. They were too bulky. Girls sure wear a lot of stuff."

"My parents say the uniform saves them money. They

don't have to buy us so many clothes. Pull up your socks, Peter. We've got seven flights of steps to climb."

"Seven?"

"We can't very well use the elevator. Someone might recognize us."

"I thought you said my disguise was perfect."

"We don't want to press our luck."

Huffing and puffing, Alice and Peter reached the seventh floor. Alice opened the stairwell door and peered into the hallway. The coast was clear. Alice led Peter to the art room, which was empty. Peter looked around. Although it was almost dark, Peter was impressed.

"This is a very nice art room," he observed. "Where are the owls?"

"Not yet, Peter. I think we should wait until it's almost dark. Otherwise we risk being seen. Let's hide behind the divan." Alice led Peter around the standing mannequin.

"We won't have long to wait. It's getting dark already."

Alice checked her watch. 5:00 PM. "You can see the owls up there on the shelf. One of them is solid gold. It's been painted over. It has to be one of those three on the far left."

"It does? Why?"

"Because they match the ones we saw in the museum. The others all have their wings in different positions."

Peter was having trouble getting settled. "How do you sit on the floor in a skirt, Alice? Pants are easier."

"Indian-style," Alice replied. "Just pull the skirt over your knees. Since you're not wearing gym shorts, you should be sure and cover up your underpants."

Peter squirmed.

Alice darted out from behind the divan. She took the beige parasol from the standing mannequin and rejoined Peter. "Here, hold this." Alice gave Peter the parasol.

"If you think I'm carrying this around, you've got another thing coming."

"It's just to block the light. So we can use the flashlight. There are no blinds on the windows and we don't want to be seen from across the street."

By then it was almost dark in the art room. The only light came from a distant street light and other buildings, which cast eerie shadows across the room.

Alice unzipped her knapsack and took out the silver nutpick.

Peter stared at the shelf of owls. "Are you sure one of them is gold. It must be worth a fortune."

"It is. That's why we've got to be careful."

"Alice," Peter said, his voice quavering. "You don't think someone will come for the owl tonight, do you?"

"Of course not. How would anyone get in the building?"

"I got in."

"That's different," Alice said. "Now I'm going to get those owls. But you'll have to turn off the flashlight because you'll need two hands to help."

"Why can't we just turn on the light?"

"Because someone will see it and think we're burglars and call the police."

"But how will we *see*?"

"Peter, there's enough light. We can do it."

"No, we can't."

Alice ignored Peter's remark. "Come and hold the ladder, Peter."

There was a crash as Peter clambered out from behind the divan. "Alice! I think there's a corpse in here."

"Don't be silly. That's a mannequin. We use it for a model and dress it in different costumes."

"No wonder it's so hard. It fell off the couch."

Peter stumbled over to the ladder.

Alice climbed to three rungs from the top and reached out for an owl. "Here, Peter," she said and handed it down to him. "We'll try this one first."

Alice climbed down the ladder. She sat with Peter behind the divan. He had picked up the flashlight and parasol again. Alice used her nutpick to scratch the owl's shoulder.

Peter held the flashlight and the parasol.

"Peter, keep the light still. Look! I think this is the one! There are yellow streaks under the blue paint. And the eyes are emeralds!" Alice contemplated her discovery. "This is it, Peter! We've got it! The case is solved, the clues are cracked. This calls for a snack."

"I'm glad you mentioned it, Alice. I'm starving."

"Hard work and excitement always make you hungry. We need to raise our blood sugar levels so we can keep up our energy."

Peter got out his thermos and took a sip of water. Alice had brought peanut butter and jelly sandwiches. She gave Peter one. She also had a large box of raisins for energy. She gave Peter a handful and stuffed her uniform pockets with the rest.

"Alice!" Peter whispered suddenly. "Stop chewing a minute! I heard a noise!"

"Oh, gosh!" Alice said, quickly swallowing. She listened. Footsteps! Soft, but definitely footsteps. Good thing they were already behind the divan, she thought. "Quick! Turn off the flashlight!"

Peter did.

"Don't move, Peter."

The footsteps came closer. The art room door opened. Whoever belonged to the footsteps had a flashlight. He moved it around and shined its beam on every object in the room. Then the light caught the ladder and followed it up to the shelf of owls.

Alice saw the person with the flashlight walk toward the ladder. She could just make out his silhouette. It was Black Hat! *Why,* she wondered, *isn't he in jail?*

Alice and Peter watched Black Hat climb the ladder. Alice gave Peter a nudge.

Peter nodded.

When Black Hat reached the top of the ladder, Alice and Peter leaped up from behind the divan and let out a whoop. They grabbed the bottom rung of the ladder and pulled. The ladder crashed to the floor.

"Quick, Peter. The flashlight."

"I think he's dead."

"Don't be silly. He's unconscious. He's still breathing. Now for the rope."

"What for?"

"We can't just go home and leave him here. He's a major suspect. We have to tie him up."

Peter got the rope from his knapsack and helped Alice tie up their victim. Alice gave the knots a few extra tugs to make sure they were secure. She decided she'd have to learn sailing and really become a knot expert.

"Now the gag, Peter."

"What gag?"

Alice hadn't thought to bring a gag. "Your sock, Peter. Take it off and stuff it in his mouth."

"What's wrong with *your* sock, Alice?"

"They *are* my socks," Alice pointed out. "In fact, take them both off. One goes *in* his mouth and the other we tie around his head."

Peter took off his socks and handed them to Alice. "You gag him. I have to put my shoes back on."

Alice did so. "A very professional job," she declared. "Now we better call the police."

"How?"

"First we get our knapsacks. I'll take the owl. Then we go down to the pay phone on the ground floor and dial nine-one-one."

CHAPTER TWELVE

A NEW DEVELOPMENT

Alice and Peter rushed through the art room door.

"Slow down, Peter. No one's chasing us. Unless Black Hat is a magician, he won't untie himself for a long time— a lot longer than it will take us to call the police. Come on."

Flashlight in one hand, the golden owl in the other, and her knapsack slung over her shoulders, Alice led Peter down the corridor toward the staircase. The public telephones were on the ground floor, off the main hall. Alice turned on her flashlight. She didn't care who saw them then. In fact, she hoped someone would see the beam of light and call the police for them.

Alice pushed the stairwell door open. She was blinded by a sudden light in her eyes. She stopped short, and Peter bumped into her again.

"Who's that?"

Alice recognized the voice. It belonged to Miss Slade! Her husband was right beside her.

Alice breathed a sigh of relief. "Miss Slade," she began, "you'll never guess what happened. This is Peter. We just caught the man who was arrested last Friday. He came back for the owl." Alice handed the statue to Miss Slade. "It's the one that was stolen. It's gold under the paint. It shows through where I scratched it. And the eyes are emeralds. And we tied up the man. He's still in the art room."

Miss Slade looked surprised. Her eyebrows shot up. "What? The gold owl? In my art room? How extraordinary! Are you absolutely sure?"

"Yes, Miss Slade," Alice said. "Look where I scratched the shoulder."

Miss Slade peered at the statue. "Look, Roger." She handed it to her husband. "I think you're right, Alice. This is very serious."

"We have to call the police," Peter said.

"Yes. We must. But first we'd better put the statue in a safe place. It's very valuable, and other people may be after it, too."

Alice knew that Miss Slade was probably right.

"I think we should get out of here," Peter said.

"We will," Miss Slade agreed, "right after we hide the statue in a safe place and call the police. I know the perfect place. The art storage room in the basement is very secure. And I have a key to it."

Alice and Peter followed Miss Slade and her husband down the stairs, which were lit only by the flashlight. They didn't want to alert any of Black Hat's accomplices who might still be in the building. Alice was thinking about the headlines in the next day's paper: "ALICE WHIPPLE FOILS THIEF."

Miss Slade pushed open the heavy door to the basement. A rush of hot air greeted them. Alice and Peter heard the furnace. Miss Slade fished in her handbag. She pulled out a ring of keys and sorted through them until she came to a large, old-fashioned one. "It's this way." She walked to the far end of the boiler room toward a row of doors. Each was identified by a sign. Miss Slade stopped at the door marked Art. She unlocked it and pushed it open.

Alice felt the firm grip of the Beard as he grabbed her wrist. She heard a click as she dropped the flashlight. Peter struggled beside her. Together they were shoved forward into the dark room. Alice realized that she and Peter had been handcuffed to each other, her left hand to his right.

"This is where we part company." Miss Slade's tone had suddenly become sinister. Her husband laughed as he pulled the door closed. Alice heard the key turn in the lock. "Bye, bye, children," Miss Slade called through the door. "In exactly three hours we will be flying over Miss Barton's on our way out of the country. We'll be sure to wave."

"Alice, would you please tell me what is going on," Peter demanded. "You said Black Hat was the thief. I want to get out of here and go home."

"You're absolutely right, Peter. This proves that my first hunch was correct. It was Miss Slade and the Beard after all."

"What about the man in the art room?"

"He must be in on it, too. You know that a lot of different people were after the Maltese Falcon."

"Well, that's just great, Alice. What do we do now?"

They heard the sound of retreating footsteps. "I can't see a thing. How are we going to get out of here?"

"Calm down, Peter." Alice hoped she sounded calm

herself. And stop moving your arms. This handcuff hurts. Our eyes will get used to the dark in a few minutes. Look! There's a window."

"Ow! Alice, stop pulling me. I'm sure glad I'm not a Siamese twin," Peter said.

"Come over here, Peter. I want to look at the window. I think it's the way we're going to escape. Miss Slade isn't so smart after all."

Alice and Peter groped their way toward the window. They had to be careful not to knock over the cardboard boxes stacked on the floor.

"I can see the moon." Alice peered through the wire mesh grating that covered the window. But then her heart sank. At least sixty feet below she saw the swirling water of the East River. It was a sheer drop. They would never escape that way. One side of Miss Barton's was built on top of the concrete wall of the riverbank. It was just their luck to be stuck in a storeroom on that side. Alice knew she would have to think of something else.

"Now what, Alice?"

"We're going to sit down and think."

"I'm not sitting down," Peter declared. "I bet there are lots of mice and rats in this basement. They probably scamper up the side of the building from the river. I don't want to get plague. You sit down."

"Peter, you know very well that I can't sit down on the floor unless you sit down. We are handcuffed together. How about if we sit on a box?"

"No box, either. Rats and mice get into boxes, too. And there's probably millions and trillions of cockroaches everywhere."

"Peter, we have to plan our escape. We can't stay here all night. Our parents won't know what happened to us. I said I'd be home right after dinner. Miss Slade and the Beard will leave the country. And we'll never find the golden owl again."

"We could signal the boats going up and down the river," Peter suggested.

Alice thought for a moment. "You know, Peter, that's not such a bad idea. Fortunately, I've got my silver nutpick in my pocket. If we remove the grating from the window, then we can open it and hang out an SOS sign."

"It's dark out, Alice. I don't think anyone will see the sign."

"We're in the art storage room. There must be some luminous paint that will catch the moonlight."

Carefully trying to avoid whatever little creatures might have been disturbed by their intrusion, Alice and Peter inspected the boxes. They found one that contained jars of paint.

"I can't see very well," Peter said. He squinted at the labels.

"Well, let's take the grating off the window. Then we'll have more light."

"That's true, I guess. Come on." Peter gave Alice a tug and they moved back to the window.

"My right hand is free," Alice pointed out. "Stand very still while I work on the grate." Alice felt around the edges of the grate and found the screws that held it in place. She pushed the nutpick into the slit on the head of one screw and turned it until the screw came out and fell to the floor.

"Hurry up, Alice."

"I *am* hurrying. The screws must be rusty."

"Probably the sea air," Peter said. "It makes things rust faster."

"Hold still, you're making my hand slip."

Finally, after what seemed like hours, Alice felt the grate move.

"Quick, Peter, your free hand! Hold up your end while I take out the last screw."

When they had the grate off the window, they stared out at the river, hoping to see some boats.

"Now there's more light," said Alice. She and Peter returned to the storage boxes and took out a spray can of bright luminous yellow paint. They found some large sheets of paper and some scotch tape.

Alice sprayed an SOS, one letter per sheet of paper. Peter helped her tape the three sheets together so that they formed a vertical banner:

$$
\boxed{\begin{array}{c} S \\ \hline O \\ \hline S \end{array}}
$$

"Now for the window," Alice said.

"If we open the window, there won't be anything to keep out the rats," Peter said.

"There are no rats, Peter."

"It's going to get cold in here with the window open," Peter pointed out. "Especially in a skirt."

"Girls wear skirts all winter. Besides, this is an emergency. Do you or do you not want to get out of here in time to warn the police that the suspects are leaving the country?"

"I guess I do."

"Well then, you're going to have to help me push up this window."

Peter and Alice pushed as hard as they could. The window went up a few inches.

"It won't go any higher, Peter. It's going to fall. Quick! Give me your shoe! We'll use it to keep the window propped up. There's just enough room to get the SOS banner through."

Peter took off his shoe and gave it to Alice.

She jammed the shoe into the opening.

"Uh-oh," Alice muttered.

"What's the matter now?"

"Your shoe fell out the window, Peter. It just sort of dropped."

"That's great, Alice." Peter was really mad. "Now what am I going to do?"

"Give me the other one."

"That's not funny."

"Listen, Peter, we've made *fantastic* progress. Now that we have the SOS banner, we just have to hang it out. I won't drop this one, I promise. Before long a passing barge will see our banner and we'll be saved."

Peter handed her the shoe, and together they hung up the banner. "I have another idea," Peter said.

"You do?" Alice was pleased with herself for having

selected such an able assistant on her first case. It made her realize that she had a natural talent for detection.

"Yes," Peter said, putting his only shoe back on his foot. "If we tap on one of the pipes down here the sound will carry upstairs to the other floors in the building.

"Who's going to hear the tapping?"

"There's got to be a night watchman in the building or someone cleaning or a teacher working late. But we need a pipe that goes straight up."

"There's a pipe in the corner. But how will anyone know it's us down here and not just a pipe banging?"

"Because, Alice. I happen to know Morse code." Peter stood with his bare foot resting on his shoe.

"You do? That's wonderful. Come on!" Alice yanked Peter over toward the corner.

"Hey! Not so fast." Peter fell against the wall. His shoulder bumped something small and sharp. "Ouch! Alice—"

"What?"

"I just bumped into a light switch."

"A what?"

"A light switch, Alice. All this time we could've had the lights on." Peter flicked the switch, and the storage room lit up.

"Well, that's a big improvement." Alice blinked to accustom her eyes to the light.

"Now we can do two kinds of Morse code," Peter said. "You do the lights on and off, and I'll tap the pipe."

"I don't know Morse code," Alice admitted reluctantly.

"It won't take you long to learn," Peter said, feeling generous. "I'll teach you SOS in Morse code and we'll signal together. You can follow me."

If Alice and Peter stretched, Alice could reach the light switch and Peter the pipe without the handcuffs cutting their wrists. Peter tapped a few times while Alice listened. Once she got the hang of the code, she flicked the light switch on and off, matching Peter's taps.

"My arm's getting tired," Peter complained after forty-five minutes.

"Okay. Two minutes rest." Alice checked her watch. "It's 7:30 PM, Peter. We don't have much time. Their plane leaves in a couple of hours."

Alice and Peter walked toward each other and let their arms drop. They shook them to loosen their muscles. Then they resumed their positions.

Alice and Peter were concentrating on their signals when the sound of footsteps echoed outside the storeroom door.

"Peter! Listen! I think our messages have finally been received."

Alice and Peter rushed to the door to welcome their rescuer. Peter didn't even mind that his bare foot had gotten quite cold.

They banged and yelled. A key turned in the lock and the door was thrust open.

Alice and Peter gasped.

Framed by the door was Black Hat.

Alice grabbed the spray paint. She aimed it directly at Black Hat and pressed. Then she saw three more men with black hats and black, belted raincoats behind him. She realized that she didn't have enough paint for all of them.

CHAPTER THIRTEEN
A CASE OF MISTAKEN IDENTITY

On the whole, Alice was pleased with the newspaper account of her first case. Miss Slade and the Beard had been arrested just before take-off and were in police custody.

She had been right about the necklace all along. The Beard turned out to be head of an international ring of thieves after all. He had stolen the owl in the museum and the necklace on a trip to South-America. His wife, Sally Slade, was his accomplice.

Alice was gratified to have been referred to in all the papers and on television as "a promising young detective." Her only regret was having sprayed bright yellow luminous paint all over the F.B.I. agent who had come to their rescue. He had been tracking the Beard and Miss Slade for several months.

Fortunately, the F.B.I. agent never realized that Alice and Peter had knocked him over when he was on the ladder. The newspaper account ended by saying that the two powerful midgets who had attacked and tied up the F.B.I. agent in the art room of Miss Barton's School for Girls were still at large.